Maximilian Schele de Vere, Gustave Doré, M. Xavier

The Myths of the Rhine

Maximilian Schele de Vere, Gustave Doré, M. Xavier

The Myths of the Rhine

ISBN/EAN: 9783337194277

Printed in Europe, USA, Canada, Australia, Japan

Cover: Foto ©Andreas Hilbeck / pixelio.de

More available books at **www.hansebooks.com**

ELECTROTYPED AND PRINTED BY
H. O. HOUGHTON AND COMPANY.

I.

II.

III.

IV.

VIII.

IX.

X.

XI.

I.

I.

THE RHINE is born in Switzerland, in the Canton of Grisons; it skirts France and passes through it, and after a long and magnificent career it finally loses itself in the countless canals of Holland; and yet the Rhine is essentially a German river.

Already in the earliest ages, long before towns were built on its banks, it saw all the Germanic races dwell here in tents, watch their flocks, and fight their interminable battles, although the clash of arms and the blast of trumpets never for a

moment aroused the impassive historian from his deep slumbers.

His silence, long continued into later centuries, does not prevent us from supposing, however, that the Rhine was already at that time the great high-road on which the Germanic races wandered to and fro, and other races came to their native land. It was the Rhine that brought to them commerce and civilization; but on the Rhine came also invasions of a very different kind. We can allude here only to those religious invasions which are connected with our subject.

In the earliest ages the South of Europe alone was inhabited, while the Northern part was covered with vast forests, as old as the world, and as yet unbroken by the footsteps of men. Dark, dismal solitudes, consisting of ancient woods or wretched morasses, where trees struggled painfully for existence and only the strongest survived when they reached the light and the sun; densely wooded deserts, in which vast herds of wild beasts pursued each other incessantly, while in the deep shadow of impenetrable foliage flocks of timid, trembling birds sought a refuge against hosts of voracious birds of prey. Thus, even while Man was yet absent, War was already reigning supreme here, and in these vast regions the Great Destroyer seemed to revel in it, as if it had been a feast, a necessity, a glory!

Had never human eye yet looked upon these magnificent but unknown regions?

Then, one fine day a host of savages appeared here and settled down with their flocks. After them came another host of more warlike and better armed men, who drove out the first comers and took possession of the tilled ground.

After them another race, and then still another. Thus it went on for years and for centuries, and all these waves of immigration came down from the extreme North, marking each halting place by a bloody battle, while the conquered people, driven by the sharp edge of the sword to seek new homes, by turns pursued and pursuing, went and peopled those wild unsettled countries which afterwards became known as Belgium and France, as Bretagne and England. Continuing their march from thence southward, from the Rhine to the Mediterranean, they spread right and left, east and west, and crossed the Pyrenees and the Alps, making themselves masters on one side of Iberia, and on the other side of the plains of Lombardy, thus changing from fugitives into conquerors.

These conquered conquerors, driven from their own homes, and now driving other nations from

their homes, these first pioneers who laid open one unknown country after another, were all children of one great family and all bore the same name of *Celts*.

But where was the first source from which this

flood of families, of peoples, of nations, broke forth,
that now overflowed Europe and in successive waves
spread over the greater part of the Old World?
Whence came these vast multitudes of Northern
visitors, unexpected and unknown, who broke the
mournful silence that had so long reigned in Europe? Were the frozen regions of the North pole,
at that early time, really so fertile in men? We
call upon men of science to answer our question.
The question is a serious one, perhaps an indiscreet
one, for who can be appealed to on such a difficult
point? History? It did not exist. Monuments,
written or sculptured? The Celts had never dreamt
yet of writings or of carvings. Does this universal
silence put it out of the power of our learned men
to give a reply? Must they confess that they are
unable to do so? By no means. Learned men
never condescend to make such confessions. The
Celts have left as a monument, a language, a dia-
lect, still largely used in certain parts of ancient
Bretagne as well as in the Principality of Wales.

Illustrious academicians, mostly Germans, did not
hesitate to go to school once more in order to learn
Breton. The self-denial of which science is capable,
deserves our admiration.

After long labors, devoted to the separation of
what belonged to the primitive language from sub-
sequent additions, our great scholars found them-

selves once more face to face with Sanskrit, the
sacred idiom of the Brahmins, the ancestor of the
old German tongue, and of the old Celtic tongue,
and thus of the Breton.

The matter was decided, scientifically and cate-
gorically, and no appeal allowed. The Celts were
a people from India. Europeans are all descended
from Indians, driven from home by some powerful
pressure, a political or religious revolution, or one
of those fearful famines which periodically devastate

that immense and inexhaustible storehouse of nations.

At first, we good people, artists, poets, or authors,
who generally claim to possess some little knowledge, were rather surprised at such a decision. But
the wise men had said so; Bengal and Bretagne
had to fraternize; the Brahmins of Benares speak
Breton and the Bretons of Bretagne speak Sanskrit.
Bretagne is Indian and India is Breton.

Comparative Philology has taught the children
of our day, that two syllables which are identical

in the idioms of two different races, prove the
connection between two nations; hybridism means
kinship.

What happy people scholars are! They can converse with people who have been dead these three
thousand years, and the grave has no secrets for
them! A single word bequeathed to us by an extinct people, enables them to reconstruct that whole
race.

But I am bound to ask them another question,
a question of much greater importance to myself.
What were the religious convictions of these first
inhabitants of Europe? I am answered by Mr.
Simon Pelloutier, a minister of the Reformed Church
in Berlin, of French descent, who has studied the
primitive creed of the Celts most thoroughly and
successfully. He tells us that these people, before
they had Druids, worshipped, or rather held in honor
the sun, the moon, and the stars, a kind of Sabaism,
which, however, did not exclude the belief in a God,
who was the creator, but not the ruler, of all things.

This god appears to me to have been very im-
perfect; he was heavy, sleepy, and shapeless, having
neither eyes to see nor ears to hear; he was incapable of feeling pity or anger, and the prayers
and vows of men were unable to reach him. Invisible, intangible, and incomprehensible, he was
floating in space, which he filled, and which he

animated without bestowing a thought upon it;
omnipotent and yet utterly inactive, creating islands
and continents, and causing the sun and the stars
to give light by his mere approach, this divine
idler had created the world, but declined taking the
trouble of governing his creation.

To whom had he confided the control over the
stars in heaven? Mr. Pelloutier himself never could
find out. As to the government of the earth, he
had entrusted it to an infinite number of inferior
deities, gods and sub-gods, of very small stature.
They were as shapeless and as invisible as he was,
but vastly more active, and endowed with all the
energy which he had disdained to bestow upon
himself. By their numbers and by their collective
force they made up for their individual feebleness
— and they must have been feeble indeed, since
their extremely small size permitted a thousand of
them to find a comfortable shelter under the leaf
of a walnut tree!

Besides, they presided over the different depart-
ments which were assigned to them, not by hun-
dreds, but by myriads, nay, by millions of myriads.
Thus they rushed forth in vast hosts, stirring the
air in lively currents, causing the rivers and brooks
to flow onwards, watching over fields and forests,
penetrating the soil to great depths, creeping in
through every crack and crevice, and breaking out

again through the craters of volcanoes. They formed a belt from the Rhine to the Taunus mountains, dazzling the whole region for a moment by a shower of sparks, and falling back upon the plain in the form of columns of black smoke.

Science has, moreover, established this incontestable principle, that motion can only be produced in two ways here. below: either by the acts of living beings, or by the contact of these microscopic deities.

Whenever the waters rose or broke forth in cataracts, whenever the leaves trembled in the wind, or the flowers bent before a storm, it was these diminutive gods who, invisible and yet ever active, forced the waters to come down in torrents, drove the tempest through the branches, bent the flowers down to the ground, and chased the dust of the highroads in lofty columns up to the clouds. It was they who caused the golden hair of the maid to fall down upon her shoulders as she went to the well, who shook the earthenware pitcher she carried on her shoulder, who crackled in the fire on the hearth, and who roared in the storm, or the eruptions of fiery mountains.

When I think of this little world of tiny insect gods, who passed through the air in swarms, coming and going, turning to the left and to the right, struggling and striving above and beneath (I ask

their pardon for comparing these deities to humble
insects, born in the mud and subject to infirmity
and death like ourselves), I cannot help thinking
of the beautiful lines by Lamartine, in which he so
graphically describes life in Nature.

" Chaque fois que nos yeux, pénétrant dans ces ombres,
De la nuit des rameaux éclairaient les dais sombres,
Nous trouvions sous ces lits de feuille où dort l'été,
Des mystères d'amour et de fécondité.
Chaque fois que nos pieds tombaient dans la verdure
Les herbes nous montaient jusques à la ceinture,
Des flots d'air embaumé se répandaient sur nous,
Des nuages ailés partaient de nos genoux ;
Insectes, papillons, essaims nageants de mouches,
Qui d'un éther vivant semblaient former les couches,
Ils montaient en colonne, en tourbillon flottant,
Comblaient l'air, nous cachaient l'un à l'autre un instant,
Comme dans les chemins la vague de poussière
Se lève sous les pas et retombe en arrière.
Ils roulaient : et sur l'eau, sur les prés, sur le foin,
Ces poussières de vie allaient tomber plus loin ;
Et chacune semblait, d'existence ravie,
Epuiser le bonheur dans sa goutte de vie,
Et l'air qu'ils animaient de leurs frémissements
N'était que mélodie et que bourdonnements."

Such were the gods known to the first ingen-
uous dwellers on the banks of the Rhine — gods
worthy of a society but just beginning. And still,
I venture to make a suggestion, which Mr. Simon
Pelloutier, my guide up to this point, has unfortunately neglected to make. It is this: I feel as if

there was hidden beneath this primitive and apparently puerile mythology a hideous monster, writhing in fearful threatenings and bitter mockery. This god Chaos, so careless and reckless, gifted with the power of creation but not with love for his work, seems to me nothing else but Matter, organizing itself. I have called these countless inferior deities microscopic. I should have called them molecular, for they are atoms, the monads of our science. There is evidently here a germ, not of a religious creed so much as of a philosophic system, a shadow of the materialism of a former civilization that is now degraded and nearly lost.

At first I doubted the correctness of the opinions of our learned men; but I begin to believe in them; yes, these early Celts had come to us from distant India, from that ancient, decayed country, and in their knapsacks they had brought with them, by an accident, this fragment of their symbolic cosmogony, the sad meaning of which was, no doubt, a mystery to them also.

After some years, perhaps after some centuries, — for time does not count for much in those questions, — the Celts became weary of this selfish Deity, which was lost in the contemplation of its own being and dwelt in the centre of a cold and empty heaven, and they desired to establish some relations between him and themselves. Unable to appeal to the Creator, they appealed to Creation, and asked for a mediator, who should hear their complaints or accept their thank-offerings and transmit them to the Supreme Power.

We have already seen that they turned first to sun and moon; but they were ill rewarded for their efforts. These heavenly bodies were either too far removed from their clients to hear their complaints, or they were too busy with their own daily duties; at all events they shared with their common master in his indifference towards men.

Our pious friends were offended by this want of consideration, and thought of looking for other intercessors, who might be less busy; whom they might not only see with their eyes but touch with their hands, and who would remain as much as possible in the same place, so as to be always on hand when they were needed.

They appealed to rivers and mountains; but the rivers had nothing permanent but their banks, and went their way like the sun and moon; while the mountains, besides being the home of wolves, bears, and serpents, and thus enjoying an evil reputation, were continually hid by snow and rain from the eyes of the petitioners.

At last they turned to the trees, and as it always happens, they now found out that they ought to have commenced where they ended.

A tree was an excellent mediator; standing between heaven and earth, it clung to the latter by
its roots, while its trunk, shaped like an arrow,
feathered with verdure, rose upwards as if to touch
the sky.

The worship of trees was probably the first effect
of sedentary life adopted by the Celts after their
long, more or less forced wanderings; in a few
years it prevailed on both sides of the river Rhine.

There was no lack of trees; every man had his
own. As he could not carry it away with him, he
became accustomed to live by its side.

Man could lean his hut against the trunk; the
flock could sleep in its shade.

The birds came to it in numbers. If they were
singing, it was a sign of joy to come; if they built
their nests there, it was an invitation to marry.

The fruit-bearing tree suggested comfort, abundance, and enjoyment; it spoke of harvest feasts
and cider-making, when friends gathered around it,
holding in their hands large horns filled to over-
flowing with foaming drink.

Soon it became customary to plant at the birth
of a child a tree which was to become a companion and a counsellor for life.

Thus in the course of time a copse represented
a family.

The worship bestowed upon the tree consisted

2

in pruning it, in making it grow straight, in freeing
its bark from parasitical growth and in keeping the
roots free from ants, rats, snakes and all dangerous
enemies.   Such continuous care naturally led in the
course of time to an improvement in cultivation.

The tree worshippers, however, did more than
this.   On certain hallowed days they hung bouquets
of herbs and of flowers on its branches, they brought
food and drink, and thus fetichism crept in gradually.   Alas!   That men have never been able to
keep from extremes !

When the wind whispered in the leaves, the devout owner listened attentively, trying anxiously to
interpret the mystic language of his cedar or his
pear tree, and often a regular conversation ensued.

It was a bad omen when a rising storm shook
the tree fiercely; if the tempest was strong enough
to break a branch, the event foretold a great calamity, and if it was struck by lightning, the owner
was warned of his approaching death.   The latter
was resigned; he felt quite proud at having at last
compelled his indolent god to reveal himself to his
devout worshipper.

When a child died, it was buried under its own
tree, a mere sapling. . But it was not so when a
man died.

The Celts used various and strange means for
the purpose of disposing of the remains of their

"A HORRIBLE CUSTOM!" (p. 21.)

deceased friends. In some countries they were burnt, and their own tree furnished the fuel for the funeral pile; in other countries the *Todtenbaum* (Tree of the Dead), hollowed out with an axe, became the owner's coffin. This coffin was interred, unless it was intrusted to the current of the river, to be carried God knows where! Finally, in certain localities there existed a custom — a horrible custom! — of exposing the body to the voracity of birds of prey, and the place of exposure was the top of the very tree which had been planted at the birth of the deceased, and which in this case, quite exceptionally, was not cut down.

Now, observe, that in these four distinct methods by which human remains were restored to the four elements of air and water, earth and fire, we meet again the four favorite ways of burial still practiced in India, as of old, by the followers of Brahma, Buddha, and Zoroaster. The fire-worshippers of Bombay are as familiar with them as the dervishes who drown children in the Ganges. Thus we have here four proofs, instead of one, of the Indian origin of our Celts. For my part at least, I confess I am convinced by this quadruple evidence.

It is to be presumed that the use of Dead Men's Trees and of posthumous drownings continued for centuries in ancient Gaul as well as in ancient Germany. About 1560 some Dutch laborers found, in examining a part of the Zuyder Zee, at a great depth, several trunks of trees which were marvelously well preserved and nearly petrified. Each one of these trunks had been occupied by a man, and contained some half-petrified fragments. It was evident that they had been carried down, trunk and man, by the Rhine, the Ganges of Germany.

As recently as 1837 such *Todtenbaume* or Dead Men's Trees, well preserved by the peculiar nature of the soil, have been discovered in England, near Solby in Yorkshire, and still more recently, in 1848, on Mount Lupfen in the Grand Duchy of Baden.

In face of such well authenticated evidence of Dead Men's Trees having been confided to the current of rivers or the bosom of the earth, it seems superfluous to ask for additional proof in support of the fact that cremation was practiced all over ancient Europe. Nor do I consider myself, as a collector of myths, bound to prove everything. I do not mean to speak, therefore, any further of Birthday Trees, of Dead Men's Trees, and of Fetich Trees, — which we shall moreover meet again presently, — and hasten on to other myths of far greater importance.

The Druids now appear for the first time in Gaul and in Germany.

II.

II.

The Druids and their Creed. — *Esus.* — *The Holy Oak.* — *The Pforzheim Lime Tree.* — *A Rival Plant.* — *The Mistletoe and the Anguinum.* — *The Oracle at Dodona.* — *Immaculate Horses.* — The Druidesses. — *A late Elector.* — *Philanthropic Institution of Human Sacrifices.* — *Second Druidical Epoch.*

The Druids were the first to bring to the Gauls as well as to the Germans religious truths, but their creed can be appreciated from no dogma of theirs; it must be judged by their rites.

The first question is: Whence did the Druids

come? Were they disciples of the Magi, and did
they come from Persia? Such an origin has been
claimed for them: or had they been initiated by Isis
in her ancient mysteries, and did they come from
Egypt? This view also has its adherents. Or,
finally, had they been driven towards Western Europe by one of the last waves of immigration, which
left India under the pressure of some new calamity? Many think so.

As it seems to be difficult to decide between these
three suggestions, it might be worth while to try and
reconcile them with each other. It is a long way
from India to Germany and to Gaul, and there might
have been many stopping places between the country
from which they started and their future home.

The Druids, like all other Celts, might very well
have started from India, and choosing not the most
direct way might have reached Europe only after
making many a long halt in Persia and in Egypt.

'If that can be admitted, then there is no difficulty
in assuming that the first Celts might very well have
taken with them from the banks of the Indus and
the Ganges only a few fragments of a sickly materialism taught by false teachers outside of the temple,
while the Druids might have been initiated within
the temple itself, thus learning to know the true
nature of the Deity.

Their creed was founded upon a triple basis — one

God; the immortality of the soul; and rewards
and punishments in a future life.

These sound doctrines, which are as old as the
world and form the foundation of all human morality,
had ever been maintained by their wise men.

At a later period the Greeks, proud as they were
of their Platonic philosophy, had not hesitated to
acknowledge that they had obtained the first germ
of it from the Celts, the Galati, and consequently
from the Druids. One of the Fathers of the
Church, Clement of Alexandria, openly admits that
these same Celts had been orthodox in their religion,
at least as far as their dogmas were concerned.

By what name was the Supreme Being known to
the Druids? They called it *Esus*, which means the
Lord, or they gave it the simple designation of *Teut*
(God). Through this Teut the German races became afterwards Teutons, the sons and followers
of Teut, and even in our day they call themselves
in their own language Teutsche or *Deutsche*.

Three marvelously brief maxims contain almost
the whole catechism of the Druids: Serve God;
Abstain from evil; Be brave!

The Druids, being warriors as well as priests,
displayed in the performance of their warlike priest-
hood all the energy, the severity, and the authority
which must needs accompany such a strange com-
bination of powers.

Holding all the power of the state in their hands, and speaking in the name of God, commanding the army, controlling the public treasury, and acting not only as judges but also as physicians, they punished heresy and rebellión, and ended lawsuits as well as diseases, by the death of the person most interested.

Their laws, liberal and philanthropic in spite of their apparent severity, allowed a jury consisting of notables, to judge grave crimes; this fact of a jury suggests naturally the idea of extenuating circum- stances, and thus the criminal, escaping more read- ily than the patient, frequently got off with a fine, if he was rich, or with banishment if he was poor.

Nevertheless all the efforts of the Druids did not succeed in thoroughly eradicating Tree worship; they were thus led to adopt one tree, to the exclusion of all others, which should rally around it the scattered adoration of all the nations. This official tree, a kind of green altar, on which God manifested him- self to his priests, was an oak, a strong, vigorous oak, the king of the forests.

Thus the holy oak became known and honored; pious worshippers came by night, with torches in their hands, in long processions to present their offerings.

This usage soon became general among all Celtic nations. Around these oaks the Druids formed sacred precincts within which they lived with their families, for they were married ; but they could have

only one wife, while the other chieftains were generally polygamists.

But the oak, although thus enjoying preëminence
over all other trees, was by no means exclusively
worshipped everywhere. Perhaps from religious
antagonism, or perhaps merely from local usage,
some provinces of Gaul and of Italy preferred the
beech and the elm. In Gaul especially, the elm
prevailed over the oak, and even Christian France
still continued for a long time to plant an elm tree
before every newly built church, so as to draw God's
blessing the more surely upon it; and down to the
end of the Middle Ages courts of justice were
always held under an elm tree. Hence the curious

French proverb, which did not always have the mocking sense in which it is used nowadays, wait for me under the elm tree! (*Attendez-moi sous l'orme.*) What was then a formal summons to appear before a judge has now come to mean: Wait till doomsday.

The ash tree, also, had its worshippers among the dwellers in high northern latitudes, and it was under the dense branches of an enormous ash tree that terrible Odin and his following of deities appeared in a dark cloud.

Thus Tree worship appeared once more. It has ever since continued to flourish more or less in Germany, and even now exists to a certain extent. But it is not the oaks, nor the beech, nor the elm, nor the ash tree, which in our day receives the worship of the young especially — but the lime tree. The admirers of the lime tree carry their fervor to fanaticism and their fanaticism to murder. I had

been unwilling to believe this. But this morning
I opened my newspaper and there I found an ar-
ticle, dated December 30, 1860, and stating that a
young man from Pforzheim, in the Palatinate, at-

tempted to murder the mayor of his town by
means of a revolver, the four barrels of which were
loaded with as many leaden balls. When he was
arrested, he declared that he had personally nothing
to say against the burgomaster, but that the latter

3

had recently ordered certain lime trees to be cut down, that *the good people of Pforzheim idolized these trees*, and that he had determined to punish him for such profanation.

The paper added : " This young man belongs to an honorable family, his antecedents are excellent, and he has never shown the slightest symptom of mental derangement."

How, then does it come about that the lime tree should in our day, in the nineteenth century, call forth sentiments of such extreme violence? The reason is that Young Germany has proclaimed it to be the Tree of Love, because *its leaves are shaped like hearts.*

If I were not afraid of getting myself into trouble, having a natural horror of all firearms, and especially of four barrelled revolvers, I should mention here, that anatomists protest against this pretended resemblance of the leaf to the heart. In reality it looks much more like the ace of hearts, as it terminates below in a sharp point — but superstition prevails over anatomy, and teaches us once more that science ought not to meddle with things pertaining to love.

The Druids' Oak, although less tempting to gallant comparisons, finally excited almost equal fanaticism. Processions and sacrifices became well nigh endless; young maidens adorned it with garlands of flowers,

interspersed with bracelets and necklaces, while
warriors suspended in its branches the most precious spoil they brought home from their battles.
If a storm arose, the other trees of the forest
seemed in good faith, humbly to bow down before
their chief.

And yet it had an enemy, a fierce, relentless

enemy. An abject, little plant, unknown and miserable in appearance, came unceremoniously and
made its home on its sacred branches and even on
its august summit; there it lived on its life's blood,
feeding on its sap, absorbing its substance, threaten-

ing to impede its natural growth, and finally carrying the impudence so far as to conceal the
glossy leaves of the noble godlike tree under its
own lustreless and viscous foliage. This hostile
and impious plant was the Mistletoe, the mistletoe
of the oak (*Guythil*).

Other people, less intelligent and less sagacious
than the Druids, would have freed the tree from
this unwelcome and obnoxious visitor, by simply
climbing up and cutting off the parasite by means
of a pruning bill. This would have been irrever-
ent as well as impolitic. What would the people
have thought? The people would most assuredly
have reasoned, that the sacred tree had been rendered powerless, being unable to rid itself of its
vermin.

The Druids did much better. They treated the
mistletoe very much as we, in our day, treat a formidable member of the opposition; they gave it a
place in the sanctuary. The mistletoe was proclaimed to be an official and sacred plant, and became an essential part of their worship. When it
was to be detached from the tree, this was not
done stealthily and by a mean iron bill-hook, but
in the presence of all, amid public rejoicings and
accompanied by solemn chants. The instrument
was a golden reaping hook, and with it the *Guythil*
was carefully cut off at the base and gathered in

linen veils. These veils became henceforth sacred, and were not allowed to be used for ordinary purposes.

The Teutons who lived on the Rhine, obtained from the mistletoe a kind of glue, which they looked upon as a panacea against the sterility of women, the ravages of diseases, the effects of witchcraft,— and also as a means to catch birds.

The Gauls, on the other hand, dried it carefully and put the dust into pretty little scent-bags, which they presented to each other as New Year's Gifts on the first day of the year. Hence, in some provinces of France, the cry is

still heard, "Aguilanneuf" (*au gui l'an neuf*), "Mistletoe for New Year!"

Modern science treats mistletoe simply as a purgative, and thus attempts to prove that our ancestors showed their affection to each other by exchanging presents of violent purgatives.

The introduction of this parasite plant into the

sanctuary became, however, very soon a public benefit. For the oak-mistletoe obtained ere long considerable commercial value, and at once counterfeiters (for even under the Druids there existed such men) went to work and gathered it from other trees also, from apple trees and pear trees, from nut trees and lime trees, from beeches, elms, and even larches. The consequence was, that owners of orchards as well as owners of forests, rejoiced in the trick, at which the Druids discreetly winked; for they took advantage of the lesson.

At one time venomous reptiles had become so

numerous in the regions of the Rhine, that they caused continually serious accidents among the

people, the majority of whom lived all day long in
the open air, and did not always sleep under shelter.
During their winter sleep, these reptiles rolled
themselves up into vast balls, and became apparently glued to each other by a kind of viscous
ooze. In this state they were called by the Celts
Serpents' Eggs, or rather *Serpents' Knots*, while
the Romans called them *anguinum*.

These strange balls were used medicinally by the
Druids like the mistletoe; they employed them
even in their religious ceremonies, and soon they
became so rare, that only the wealthiest people
could procure them, by paying their weight in gold.
If the Druids had really at first been misled so as
to adopt superstitious customs, which they repented
of in their hearts, they soon found means to make
these same superstitious rites beneficial to the
people.

Unfortunately serpents' knots, oaks, and their
parasites, did not long satisfy a people ever desir-
ous of new things. It is a well-known fact that
innovations, however small may have been their
first beginning, are sure to go on enlarging and
increasing from day to day.

The old party of Tree worshippers, still numerous and very active as all old parties are, com-
plained of the suppression of their companion-trees,
the ancient family oracles, for the purpose of fa-

voring one single oak tree, — a tree which yet was
not able, in spite of all the privileges it enjoyed.
to put them into communication with *Esus*, the god
of heaven.

This complaint was certainly not unfounded; —
it had to be answered.

The Druids consisted of three classes: —

The Druids proper (*Eubages*, they were called in
Gaul) were philosophers as well as scholars, perhaps
even magicians, for magic was at that time nothing
more than the outward form of science. They
were charged with the maintenance of the principles of morality, and had to study the secrets of
nature. The Prophets, on the other hand, knew
how to interpret in the slightest breath of wind, the
language of the holy oak, which spoke to them in
the rustling of its leaves, in the soughing of the
branches, in the low cracking heard within the
trunk, and even in the earlier or later appearance
of the foliage. There were, finally, the Bards, poets
bound to the altar.

While the bards were singing around the oak,
the prophets caused it to render its oracles. These
oracles soon increased largely not only in Europe.
but also in Asia Minor, where a Celtic colony, according to Herodotus, established in the land they
had conquered the oracle of Dodona. Early Greece
worshipped an oak tree, which Strabo, however, as-

sures us was a beech. There is no disputing about trees any more than about colors; but Homer calls it an oak, and an oak it must remain for us.

This new movement, grafted upon the simple worship of the Druids, did not stop here. After

having for some time been accustomed to converse with Teut by means of a tree, the Celts were naturally surprised at seeing that, while trees could speak, living creatures remained silent, and were apparently deprived of the power of foretelling the future. Certain chieftains, especially, felt aggrieved, upon setting out on a great campaign, that they were not allowed to carry the holy oak along with them, and in their intense devotion, fell upon the idea of consulting the nervous trembling of their horses and their sudden neighing in moments of surprise or terror, — for in order to be of prophetic nature the movements of the animals had to be involuntary and spontaneous. As this creed began to spread gradually, every man who was setting out on a journey or a warlike expedition mounted his horse in the firm conviction that he would be able to consult his four-footed prophet at any time during his absence from home, provided he was able to submit the omens to the learned interpretations of a soothsayer.

The Druid priests were not long in becoming seriously alarmed at these travelling oracles, liable as they naturally were to contradict each other.

As they had before chosen a single tree to be the sacred tree, so they now accepted as genuine omens only the symptoms noticed in certain horses which were bred within the sacred precincts and under their own eyes.

These horses, of immaculate whiteness and raised at public expense, were not employed for any work, and never had to submit to saddle or bridle. Wild and untamed, they roamed with fluttering manes in perfect liberty through the lofty forests. The free-

dom of their movements gave naturally a safer
character to their omens, and thus these prophetic
horses, which formed almost a part of the druidical
clergy, enjoyed for a long time the highest authority in all Celtic countries, when suddenly one fine
day new rivals arose.

Other living creatures entered into competition
with them, and these rivals of the horses were —
shall I say it? — were women. These women
discovered, all of a sudden, that they also were
endowed, and in the very highest degree, with the
gifts of second sight, of inspiration, intuition, and
divination.

When public opinion appealed to the Druids to
give their views on this claim, they admitted, according to the statement of Tacitus, that women had
something more instinctive and more divine in them
than men, nay, even than horses. Their sensitive
organization predisposed them to receive the gift
of prophecy, and hence "women indeed act more
readily from natural impulse, without reflection,
than from thought or reason."

This last explanation, improper in the highest
degree, does not come from Tacitus, nor from myself, God forbid! It is the exclusive property of
the aforementioned Mr. Simon Pelloutier. Let
every one be responsible for his own work!

The Druids treated the women just as they had

treated the horses, the mistletoe, and the trees. They acknowledged as true prophetesses only those who were already under the direct influence of the holy place and the sacred oak; that is to say, their wives and their daughters.

The principle of centralization of power is evidently not of modern origin.

Thus, there were now Druidesses, as there had

 been Druids before. The latter became the teachers of the young men; they taught their pupils the motions of the stars, the shape and extent of the earth, the divers products of nature, the history of their ancestors written in the form of poems which the bards recited; in fact, they taught them everything except reading and writing. Memory was as yet sufficient for all things. The priestesses, on the other hand, opened schools for the young girls; they taught them to sing and to sew, they initiated them into religious ceremonies and confided to them the knowledge of simples; nor was poetry neglected, as they had to learn by heart certain poems which were specially composed for their benefit. These verses, of somewhat doubtful

lyrical character, probably taught them how to make bread, how to brew beer, and other small details of the kitchen and the house.

The 'Druidesses practiced also medicine. This threefold prerogative of being physicians, prophets, and preceptors, finally raised them so high in the estimation of the nation, that when the priests of Teut were compelled to abandon their sanctuaries, they did not hesitate to confide them to their guardianship. They even presided in their own right, at certain ceremonies.

If one of them excelled by the frequency, the lucidity, and the reliability of her inspirations, as was the case at different times with the illustrious Aurinia, Velleda, and Ganna, whom the Roman emperors even deigned to consult through their ambassadors, the proud Druids placed her with humble submission, at the head of their own college of priests. During this female dictatorship, she became the arbiter of the destiny of nations, decided on peace and war, and controlled all the movements of great armies.

Cæsar tells us that he once asked one of his German captives, why Ariovistus, their chieftain, had never yet dared to meet him in battle, and was told in reply, that the Druidesses, after a careful examination of the eddies and whirlpools of the Rhine, had forbid his engaging in action till the time of the new moon. As a matter of course, the shrewd general profited by this information, and when the new moon appeared, the Germans were in full flight.

But the Rhine has not yet given its oracles, and the time has not yet come, when Ganna, Velleda, and Aurinia condescend to grant audiences to Roman ambassadors.

We only wished to trace in a few outlines the future development of this institution of Druidesses, which we shall meet again in the days of its decline.

In the mean time, however, their influence and their power were daily growing. Were the Teutons at last satisfied? By no means. In spite of all the skill displayed by their diviners and the Druidesses, they came to the conclusion, that neither the trembling foliage of the holy oak, nor the sudden starts, the wild leaps, and the more or less prolonged, loud neighings of the horses, afforded them sufficient excitement and perfectly reliable revelations. It occurred to them next, to consult animals, not in their outward manifestations, but in their still quivering entrails. This new ceremony could not fail to give to their religious worship a more serious aspect, and a certain savor of murder, which no doubt had its charms for a warlike people.

The Druids yielded once more, but they felt discouraged. What had become of that grand philosophic religion, which was content with prayer and meditation, and which they once — too fondly, perhaps — had hoped to be able to adapt to the nature of these barbarians?

They first consented to slay at the foot of the sacred oak, so long kept free from blood, a number of noxious beasts, like wolves, lynxes, and bears; but the turn of domestic animals came ere long, and they began to sacrifice sheep, goats, and finally man's best companion in war, the horse. Not even the spotless white horses, heretofore looked upon with such profound and superstitious reverence, were spared any longer.

And at each step forward in this bloody career, the Druids, always resisting, and always compelled to yield, made their last and their very last concession, vainly hoping that they might thus retain for a little while longer the power, which they felt was fast slipping from their grasp.

Encouraged by success, the reformers finally came to the question, whether the most acceptable offering to be presented to God, was not the blood of man? Is not man, of all created beings, the most noble and the most perfect? Perhaps they were inclined to carry the argument still farther, and to reason that among all men the most worthy to be chosen and the most likely to be acceptable to God, were the Druids themselves? But they took care not to ask too much at once. They held this final consequence of a great principle in reserve, requiring for the present nothing more than a common victim, anything that might come in the way, provided it was a human being.

It might have been expected, that when this abominable demand was made to hallow murder by committing it in the name of Heaven, the descendants and heirs of the ancient sages would have remembered their noble ancestors who had put an end to the first and quite inoffensive superstitions of the early Celts. They ought to have veiled their faces, drawn back with horror, and recovering for once their former energy, appealed by means of the holy oak, the spotless horses, the soothsayers and the Druidesses, nay of heaven and earth itself, to the whole nation, calling upon them to anathematize the infamous petitioners. But they did no such thing. On the contrary they hastened to legalize such savage bloodshed by their holy consent. One might almost be led to suspect that they had themselves, underhand, suggested the horrible idea.

O ye hypocritical priests, ye false philosophers, ye tigers disguised as shepherds of the people! . . . . But we must check our indignation. For who knows, but they may have been swayed not so much by an instinct of cruelty as by a lofty political, or even philanthropic principle? Philanthropic? Yes, indeed; we will explain.

Among the Celts human life counted for little; it was lavished in battles, it was cast away in duels. At the time when the Gauls held large national assemblies, they tried to secure punctual attendance by simply putting to death the man who was the last to come; he paid for all the tardy ones. I do not mean to propose such a plan at the present day; but after all it was an infallible and economical measure.

4

The Teutons, on the other hand, bloodless in their national assemblies, after a battle in which they had been victorious, delighted in massacring all their prisoners.

These massacres ceased from the time when the Druids claimed for themselves the exclusive right of human sacrifices.

The good Esus, having become bloodthirsty, demanded all the captives to be slain in expiation at his altar, and woe to him who dared to anticipate him in his wrath. He was excluded from the sacred precincts; he was declared an impious, sacrilegious person, who could no longer take his place among the citizens; and he ran great risk of being forced to offer his own life in compensation for that which by his fault was wanting at the holocaust.

When this custom became once fully established, the prisoners of war were all delivered up to the high-priest, who chose from among them one or more to be slain as an offering. The victim was generally one of the captive chieftains, and he was slain together with his war horse, so as to add to the impressiveness of the ceremony and to reconcile the spectators by the abundance of blood that was shed to the small number of victims.

After having carefully examined the opened bodies of man and animal, the sacrificing priest, his beard and clothes saturated with blood, raised his bloody right hand to heaven and, reeking with murder and breathing carnage, he proclaimed that his god was satisfied. The remainder of the prisoners were kept for another day, but that other day never came.

Thus a new office had been created: that of a sacrificing priest. On both banks of the Rhine, in Germany as well as in Gaul, the Druids reserved this office for themselves; in other Celtic countries, in Scandinavia and among the Scythians, women performed the terrible duty; we all remember as a proof of it, Iphigenia of Tauris.

Whatever we may think of this bloody innovation, it certainly benefited the prisoners, but the Druids obtained from it, after all, the greatest advantage. Their power, which had been seriously undermined, step by step, was once more firmly established. The opposition, which had paid no attention to their remonstrances or their prayers, shrunk from their knives.

From this moment begins the Second Period of the Druids.

The bloody knife of the Druids remained long all powerful, but we need not follow its later fate. Cæsar had conquered and pacified Gaul, and the successors of Augustus fulminated their Imperial decrees against the Druids, as slayers of men, while the same knife continued to shed the blood of the Germans.

III.

III.

Any one who has ever travelled in my company, must know that I am apt to stray from my way, or at least to choose the longest route. I have a fancy to-day, to turn my eyes and my steps away from those sacred precincts of the Druids, which had become slaughter-houses and in which the hand that blessed was also the hand that killed.

I desire to breathe an air less filled with the perfumes, or rather the fetid odor of sacrifices. Up there, on that hill-top, where the setting sun lights up the bright summit, I shall breathe more freely.

Here I am.

Beneath me the Rhine spreads out its two banks, not united yet by any bridge, and even without a ferry to bring the one nearer to the other.

But on both sides, half hid under dense willow thickets and gigantic reeds, there lie, in many a shallow little bay, large numbers of tiny barks. These cunning looking boats belong to harmless fishermen in the daytime; but at night they are filled with robbers and corsairs, who form in bands, cross over to the other side in search of booty, and even venture, if needs be, out into the Northern Sea. Just now nothing stirs; the fishermen have gone home, the corsairs have not come forth. I look farther out.

On the left bank there are some Gallic Celts encamped, with blue eyes, white skin, and abundant golden tresses. Almost naked, their principal garment seems to be that immense shield, almost as long as their body, which shelters them on the march as well as when they are at rest, and which protects

them against the sun and the enemy alike. All of
a sudden I hear them, with lips held close to one
of the edges of their shields, utter sharp cries,
which are taken up and repeated, from distance to
distance, all the way down the river. To these
cries, which no doubt represent their telegraphic
system, there comes an answer from far sounding
trumpets.

Who are these other soldiers with the black hair
and the bronzed complexions? Carefully arrayed

in symmetrical lines they advance steadily, clad in
brilliant armor, and carrying banners surmounted
by golden eagles with half open wings. Has
Cæsar really succeeded, after ten years' warfare, in
making himself master of Gaul as far as the banks
of the Rhine? I cannot doubt it; for at their

approach, the Gauls lower their lance-heads, in
token of their peaceful disposition, and allow them
to pass.

When they reach the river, the small Roman
army pauses; under the protection of this armed
force a few men, dressed in simple tunics, with no

arms but tablets, a style, and ropes for measuring
the ground, go to work preparing a plan, perhaps
for a bridge, perhaps for a town.

German sentinels, take care!

From the height of my hill I look down upon a

narrow strip of land on the right bank of the river,
and here I see several groups of men, scattered
here and there in the woods and on the plain,
who work under the superintendence of a Druid.
Some are digging up the roots of trees which
overshadow or impoverish the ground; others draw
long furrows with the iron of their ploughs.
These laborers seem all to suffer from some restraint which impedes their movements, but of
which at this distance I can discover no cause.

In order to meditate on this strange sight, I
look around for a resting place. Half way up the
hill I notice a small stone bench. As I draw

nearer, the object grows in size and rises to such
a height, that I should need a ladder if I wished
to take possession of my seat.

This apparent bench is a monument, a Druidical
monument, and consists of two upright stones, on
which rests a third, horizontal stone. In France,
in England, and in Germany there are still found

such Druidical altars, cromlechs or dolmens; these menhyrs astonished already Alexander of Macedonia when he marched through Scythia. In Bretagne, at Carnac, some of these stones, consisting of a single rock, rise by the wayside, as if to tell the

traveller the story of the past, or they range themselves before his eyes in long lines, forming on the ground endless circles of emblematic meaning, as it is supposed. But the traveller can no longer understand their language. Was this an altar, or was it an idol, or perhaps only a simple monument raised over a grave. If they were altars, Carnac would be Olympus; if they were tombstones, it would be a cemetery.

I was going all around the mystic three stones to examine them more closely, when I noticed close by a flock of sheep, and then a shepherd.

This shepherd, covered with a ragged *sagum*, had on his feet leather sandals, a half open wound on his forehead, which had not yet had time to close, enhanced the fierceness of his appearance. His burning glances fell now upon the Druidical stone and now upon another object which I had not noticed before. This was the guard of a sword which had been driven into the ground.

Could it be that this sword handle, and this stone resting upon two supports, were new con- cessions made by the pol- itic Druids?

As according to their spiritualistic views God could not render himself visible in a shape resem- bling our own, they had represented him as well as they could by a sym- bol. It appeared thus that human sacrifices were al- ready no longer sufficient to maintain their creed.

While I was examining with growing curiosity this strange keeper of sheep, a young girl, tall and fair, with bare neck and bare feet, was busy watch- ing on the same side of the hill another flock, and at the same time gathering herbs for medic- inal purposes. When she was about to leave, she offered the shepherd to attend to his wound, but he refused haughtily; she ran away laughing, and threw a flower into his face.

He did not pick up that flower; he did not salute that pretty girl as she left him. He looked at her with disdain.

Ah! I can doubt it no longer; this unhappy man is like the wood-cutter in the forest, and the laborers in the field, one of those prisoners taken in war, whom the Druids have spared, and now render useful. His closely shorn hair, his open wound, and the heavy wooden yoke which he has to carry on his neck, all betray his sad fate. He has made no reply to the half pitiful, half coquettish advances of the pretty gatherer of simples, because she has only awakened in his heart painful memories of his distant love, or of his wife, whom he is never to see again! He has cast glances of fierce hatred and burning revenge at the Druidical altar and the handle of the sword, because both of these objects point out the place of bloody sacrifices. Does he think he is himself destined to be slain? or was perhaps the warrior whom they slew yesterday, a man of his own tribe, his best friend, his own brother?

But I have taken refuge here in order to escape from these painful thoughts of blood and murder. I propose to seek new objects of interest.

Farther down, nearly at the foot of the hill, I

see a few huts, or rather a few low, almost crushed roofs, which seem hardly to rise from the ground. Are they houses, or stables, or caves?

On the left bank Gauls and Romans have alike disappeared in the mists rising from the river. On the right bank the wood-cutters and the field-laborers are resting upon their axes or their ploughs,

and seem to ask the sun if the day is not drawing to an end.

A breeze is springing up, the shepherd gathers his flock and, as mournful as ever, he slowly takes the footpath that leads down the hill towards the village.

I follow him without knowing what mysterious power draws me in that direction.

Perhaps some Druid magician holds me under a potent spell, which enables me to forget who I am, whence I come, and even to what century I belong, and to witness these strange scenes, which, well nigh forgotten by all living beings, I alone am permitted to watch? Let me try, at all events, to profit by this rare piece of good fortune.

I reach the low village and find it occupied by a colony of Salic Franks, who live scattered all along the Rhine. With their eyes fixed upon the left bank, they are just now far more occupied with the invasion of Germany by the Romans, than with the thought of invading Gaul themselves.

I feel suddenly a deep interest in these people. What Frenchman of this nineteenth century can feel sure that the blood in his veins is not the same that once gave life and strength to these terrible warriors from the North, Franks or Gauls? We are all natives of one or the other bank of this great river Rhine, and feel towards each other, whether we live on the right or the left bank, very much like school-boys whose friendship is cemented by many a battle royal.

Being a Frenchman, I feel that I am about to

pay a visit to my paternal ancestors — for the
Franks have given us our name. No wonder that
I feel deeply moved.

I examine the low huts of the village, if village
it can be called, and find that they are separated
from each other by commons and by fields, and
that they finally lose themselves in the open country. Where now these scattered huts are standing,
there may be one of these days a Mayence or a
Cologne, and yet they will occupy no larger space
with all their suburbs included.

On both sides of the road extend orchards,
fenced in with reeds and all aglow with blooming
apple trees ; dark, sombre pine forests and swamps,
the greenish waters of which are confined within
slight dams ; here and there the live rock crops
out from the ground and interrupts the road, or
huge trees are lying across, recently cut down and
but just deprived of their branches. In the open
pasture grounds huge buffaloes are lying about
snorting and panting with fatigue, for they have
worked all day in the plough ; the neighing of
horses is heard from one end of the country to
the other, and gradually dies out as the sun sinks
below the horizon ; lean heifers, with long, spiral
horns, push here and there their heads through
the fence of the orchards to have a last bite at the
tender foliage of the reeds, and small oxen of an

inferior breed return to their quarters at the same time with the sheep, quite content to browse on the grass by the wayside, while herds of swine are wallowing in the mire of the low grounds.

The landscape resembles parts of Bretagne and of Normandy; but these provinces have no such huts. To see a human habitation, you have to rise high above the fences and hedges and then look down upon the ground.

At a place where two roads meet, the cracking of a whip is heard; hogs, sheep, and small oxen are driven aside to make way for a kind of procession, consisting of grave and solemn men and women, who almost all wear a look of consternation.

It is a wedding.

Two young people have just had their union blessed by the priests under the sacred oak. The bride is dressed in black, and wears a wreath of dark leaves on her head; she walks in the midst of her friends, bent double, as if weighed down by overwhelming thoughts. A matron, who walks on her left, holds before her eyes a white cloth; it is a shroud, the shroud in which she will be buried one of these days. On her right, a Druid intones a chant, in which he enumerates, in solemn rhythm, all the troubles and all the anxieties which await her in wedded life.

" From this day, young wife, thou alone wilt have to bear all the burden of your united household.

" You will have to attend the baking oven, to provide fuel, and to go in search of food; you will have to prepare the resinous torch and the lamp.

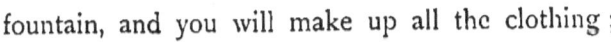

" You will wash the linen at the fountain, and you will make up all the clothing;

" You will attend to the cow, and even to the horse if your husband requires it;

" Always full of respect, you will wait upon him, standing behind him, at his meals;

" If he chooses to take more wives, you will receive your new companions with sweetness;

"If needs be, you will even offer to nurse the children of these favorites, and all from obedience to your karl (master);

"If he is angry against you and strikes you, you will pray to Esus, the only God, but you will never blame your husband, who cannot do wrong.

"If he expresses a wish to take you with him to war, you will accompany him to carry his baggage, to keep his arms in good condition, and to nurse him if he should be sick or wounded;

"Happiness consists in the fulfillment of duty. Be happy, my child!"

When I heard this dolorous wedding song, which in some parts of France is to this day addressed to brides by local minstrels, when I saw this wind-ing-sheet, the mournful costumes and the whole funereal wedding procession, I felt overcome with sadness. Just then, cries and joyous acclamations were heard at some little distance.

Another procession came from the opposite direction to the cross-roads; there all the faces were smiling and full of joyousness.

This was a funeral.

Such were the ways of our fathers; they rejoiced in facing death, which relieves man from all his sufferings; they had nothing but tears for man when he entered upon his trials.

In the meantime the twilight had passed into darkness. Small lights, looking like will-o'-the-wisps, were flitting to and fro in field and forest, going in all directions. Devout worshippers, carrying torches or lanterns in their hands, were going to consecrated places, to hold public worship or to recite private prayers.

Some, and these were the majority, go in the
direction of the oak forests, where the Druids are
found ; others, concealing the light of their lanterns
as well as they can, go hither and thither, towards
the copses of beeches and pine trees, or towards
the river, or towards the hill, which was but just
now shining brightly in the sunlight, but is now

concealed in utter darkness. What are they going
to do ? They are going to worship the Rhine, the
wells, the water-courses, the trees, the Druidical

altars, and the sword-guards. For no creed yet but
has had its schisms.

Orthodox or not, German or Gallic, the Franks
have always shown a preference for nocturnal worship; they divide the year into moons, and count
the moons not by days but by nights. And yet
they have been suspected of worshipping the sun!
And I had nearly fallen into the same error!
How well it was that I came to see for myself!

As I am just now more interested in watching
manners than in studying mythology, I pursue my
investigations, especially as I know very well that
we must know the lives which people lead in order
to be able fully to appreciate the objects of their
worship.

While all these small lights are flashing, like
shooting stars, here and there through the landscape, certain specially bright lights seem to become
stationary and permanent. These are the lighted-
up windows of human habitations. I called the
latter just now stables, or caves, and excepting a
few of them, I must still call them such.

They are dug out of the ground, damp and dark;
their ceiling is on a level with the surface of the
earth, and their roof consists of layers of turf, or of
dry thatch covered with moss. The only door
resembles the lid of a snuff-box, and is set in the
roof on a level with the ground. The dwelling

has no light but such as enters through these trap-
doors; consequently they are utterly dark during the
whole rainy season and during winter, that is to say,
for three fourths of the year! Darkness reigns supreme here; that darkness which is the enemy of
all healthfulness, of enjoyment, of every comfort.
No windows! No glass! O divine Apollo, —

"Thou of the silver bow, god of Claros, hear!"

I never had any objection to the doctrine which
made of you, the brilliant personification of the sun,

a first class divinity; but I think like honors ought
to have been bestowed upon the unknown man
who first invented windows and window-panes, the

first glazier in fine. He ought at least to have been made a demigod, and if he had to remain a simple mortal, they ought surely to have remembered his name! Alas! that high honors are as unfairly distributed in heaven as upon earth!

As there is no window, I peep through the trap-door to see how these subterranean dwellings look inside. The aspect is far from being as wretched as I had expected. I find that the walls are hung with mattings and the floor is beaten hard; by the side of the smoking lamp which is suspended from the main beam of the ceiling, there are hanging, on hooks, a hindquarter of venison, baskets filled with provisions, and implements for fishing and hunting. Besides, I notice long strings of medicinal herbs, such as we see in the shops of herb-doctors, and among these plants the mistletoe occupies, as a matter of course, the place of honor.

In another underground hut there appear actually some traces of luxury. Here the walls are incrusted with pebbles from the Rhine, of many colors and skillfully arranged; here and there weapons are arranged in various shapes; javelins with sharp hooks; framees, such as the ancient Franks were using; hatchets of stone or iron; "morning stars," with sharp points, were pleasantly mingled with huge bucklers; large leather quivers and long arrows feathered at one end and with jagged teeth at the other. At first sight it looks as if for the purpose of softening somewhat the threatening aspect of these panoplies, the Celtic lady of the house had added some of her jewels to these weapons. But it is not so; these gold chains, these necklaces set with onyx and rubies, are worn by the grim warriors on the day of battle, quite as much in the nature of ornaments as for the purpose of protection. One of our sober, I may say, most sober historians, ascribes to this custom of our forefathers, the Franks, the gorget, worn still by officers in some European armies. Here also I see straw mats, but here they are trod under foot; they are used as carpets, not as hangings.

The deep and spacious dwelling contains, besides the large room which alone I can see through my dormer-window, a number of other rooms on all sides, or rather of other caves, which are all connected with each other. I am evidently before the palace of one of the chief men of the country.

In the first hut, into which I had looked, I had found the people at table, drinking a beverage made from grain and herbs — cerevisia — in horns of wild bulls, and talking about business — for our ancestors talked about business at dinner, just as we do. The conversation turned about exchanges of rams, a great fishing expedition to be undertaken jointly, an invasion to be made into the territory on the other

turned around and around rapidly. Light red lines had already begun to mark the skin of the two adversaries; the blood was trickling down their arms, but these wounds were such trifles that the spectators took no notice of them and uttered not a single exclamation.

All of a sudden I heard three hurrahs in rapid succession; the welcomed guest, whom all had been striving to honor to the utmost of their capacity, had fallen down with his adversary's knife still sticking in his breast. He was dead.

They had not been able to think of any better way to make him spend a pleasant evening. The good old times had a hospitality of their own!

This pleasant handkerchief game has survived, only slightly modified, in several countries of northern Europe. The handkerchief is generally wrapped around a rapier, so as to shorten the length of the blade. In the taverns of Holland the game is considered conducive to health; a knife wound gives a man a chance to escape apoplexy; it serves as a timely bleeding.

I had run away in horror. For an hour I wandered about, casting a furtive glance down a trapdoor here and there, and almost everywhere I saw men and women, horses and cattle, enjoying their rest, lying pell-mell on the same litter.

In one of these hovels I thought I recognized

the young girl whom I had seen on the hill; her
attitude of repose gave a peculiar charm to her
supple and delicate limbs, and by the feeble flick-
ering light of the lamp, she suggested the idea of
a sleeping nymph.

She was a young Ionian girl, a countrywoman of
Aspasia ; captured in war, she had been sold as a

slave in twenty markets, developing in spite of such
treatment, one grace and one beauty after another.
On the banks of the Ilyssus, they would have
erected an altar in her honor, on the banks of
the Rhine they made her keep a herd of swine.

She was not the only one of her sex, however, whom I saw during that fantastic night.

The sound of a shrill fife, mingling with the sweeter notes of a harp, attracted my attention. I went toward the spot from which the music came.

In a little room decked with flowers, a young woman was engaged in her toilet.

I ought to have fled once more, — this time from bashfulness or a sense of propriety, — but a conscientious historian is bound to overcome every difficulty, in order to ascertain the exact truth. It was a great piece of good luck, surely, to be able to report as an eye-witness, what might be seen in the boudoir of a Celtic lady.

My friend was sitting, half undressed, on a stool, with her hair loosened, and holding in her hand a metal mirror. An old woman, a servant or her mother, I cannot tell which — and yet it seemed to me as if I had seen both these women, as well as the beautiful swine-herd, somewhere before; when that was, however, I could not possibly tell — the old woman held the whole rich abundance of the young lady's hair in both her hands and rubbed it with a horrid mixture of tallow, ashes, and plaster. Thanks to this wretched pomatum, the beautiful hair gradually changed from pale blonde to intense red, and thus enabled the owner to comply with a fashion, which I do not presume to criticise, but

6

simply record here. Then she washed and combed
it carefully, plaited it cunningly, and at last rubbed
the shoulders and the neck of the beauty with
melted butter, while she washed the face and the
hands with foaming beer.

After the demands of cleanliness had thus been

satisfied, she placed before her mistress a slight
collation, which was promptly served and promptly
dispatched. While she was thus attending to her
toilet and disposing of a bird's meal, there was a cy-
clopean feast going on in an adjoining room; loud
and violent voices were heard, everybody seemed

to talk at once, and in such high tones that even the shrill fife could no longer be distinguished — for it was from this hall that the sound of music proceeded, which had attracted me to the dwelling.

The old woman evidently thought the feast was drawing to an end, for she hastened to finish her mistress's toilet. She opened a wooden box and drew from it a pair of pretty red boots, which she put on the feet of the young beauty; then she threw over her white dress a purple scarf, which she fastened on the left shoulder with a long thorn from a sloe-tree. After that she tied a narrow scarlet ribbon around her head, handed her a collar and bracelets made of small berries, which in form and color were strikingly like corals, and finally, as the finishing touch, she daubed her cheeks with red by means of a cosmetic which I suspect consisted largely of brickdust. When the young Frankish beauty found that there was enough red — scarlet, crimson, purple, and pink — on her person from head to foot, she uttered a cry of triumph, especially when her husband, who entered her room, followed by his guests, seemed to be quite dazzled by the resplendent charms of his lovely wife, whom he had just *bought*.

To buy a woman was a familiar expression in Germany at that time, as it is now, — *Ein weib kaufen*. It must be borne in mind, however, that in those days the bride brought no dower; on the contrary, the husband paid her family a certain sum as compensation. We have inherited many of our usages from our Celtic forefathers; but as to this custom, we have not thought proper to keep it up.

I at once recognized the husband, although he was now all smiles in his face, and let us hope, all smiles in his heart also. He was the chief personage in the wedding procession, whom I had seen two hours before, looking so grave and solemn, so sad and mournful.

According to Druidical regulations, the bride has first of all waited upon him at table, humbly standing behind him like the other house slaves; then, towards the middle of the repast, she had gone to her room in order to exchange her girlish costume for the dress of a married woman — a woman who has the right to follow the fashions and to dress herself up in red from the heels of her feet to the end of her hair.

Now she receives her master *at home;* here she is mistress, and mistress she will remain. This was the rule among the Franks; for in spite of the lachrymose anthems of the bards and in spite of the sombre ceremonies of the wedding, the women became almost invariably the masters at home, a usage which, contrary to that of dowerless girls, may possibly have crossed the Rhine.

Thinking it over, I found that during my nocturnal excursion into the land of my forefathers, I had been present — as a witness only, be it understood — at three successive entertainments; a feast of welcome, a business dinner, and a wedding dinner. Although they had not been calculated to satisfy my appetite, they had, at all events, made me extremely hungry. I was thinking, therefore, of retracing my steps and look-ing for a lodging, when I saw the Druid-bard, who had not disdained taking a seat at the nuptial feast, coming slowly and solemnly to the centre of the room, all the while drawing a few accords from a kind of harp, which consisted of a closely bent bow with three strings instead of one.

He was getting ready to charm the company with the recital of one of those long and mysterious poems which recount the history of the Celts. I delay my departure.

It has been said, and not without a show of reason, that the history of our Gallic or Germanic ancestors ought to be for us a subject of deep interest; but bold minds have in vain tried to raise

up once more the old oak tree, to trim it and to
let air and light enter within its canopy of leaves.
The birds that once sang in its branches have left
no trace behind them of their songs, and nothing
has reached us from those sacred precincts but a
few faint echoes.

I certainly have reason to praise my good fortune ! What all these great scholars, these learned
men, have not been able to accomplish by dint of
energy and perseverance and aided by all their
knowledge of Latin, Greek, and Sanskrit, I (I, the
man whom you know) am enabled to do ! Thanks
to the bard's long recital, I am able to fill up
this blank, — the first, the only man in the history
of mankind, who can throw light upon the impenetrable darkness of those ages !

The bard began. I listened, all attention and
eagerness, trying to catch every sound and to impress every word upon my excellent memory.

In a pompous introduction he told us all about
the first arrival of the Celts in Europe, the coming
of the Druids as apostles of the true faith ; he told
us how a great colony of Salic Franks, Gauls,
under the collective name of Pelasgi, all children
of Teut, or Teutons, had first planted a sacred oak
at Dodona. On this point I was already well informed. He then alluded to the building up of
Athens, due as much to the Teutons as to the

Greeks of Cecrops; he boasted, that when the
Greeks were led astray by their corrupt imagination and wished to raise altars to Saturn, Jupiter,
and all those false gods whom they had borrowed
from the Egyptians and the Phœnicians, the Teutons rose in the name of outraged human reason,
and proclaimed the only one God, breaking down
all the false altars. Hence, he said, that formidable struggle, still so well known as the battle of
the gods of Olympus against the *Teutons* or *Titans. . . . .*

I held my breath. What ? Those terrible giants,
those colossal men, whom Jupiter himself feared
and who piled Ossa upon Pelion, or Pelion upon
Ossa — they were Celts ? They were the ancestors
of the brave French ?

O Titans, O my brothers, with what delight I
listened to the sacred words of the bard, so that I
might repeat them to you and rejoice with you in
our glorious descent!

By special grace I understood the Germano-
Celtic words of the bard without difficulty. But
the poem was flowing on interminably ; I began to
mistrust my memory. Centuries succeeded centuries, events followed events, and they were as close
to each other and as numerous as grains in a bag
of wheat. The continuous exertion of all my fac-
ulties began to tell upon me. The most illustrious

heroes of Gaul and of Germany appeared to me soon only·like the faint forms seen by means of a magic lantern; Sigovesus and Bellovesus, the descendants of the great king Ambigat; Brennus, Belgius, and Lutharius, sons or sons-in-law of that other great king Cambaules, began to turn around and around in my head, holding each other by the hand and performing an old British dance to the music of an old Breton instrument. Ariovistus played on the *biniou.* Then the sounds of the biniou, the shrill tones of the fife and the Druid harp were broken in upon by a terrible noise of countless church bells; the air shook all of a sudden, the earth trembled, everything around me fell to the ground with a great crash, the Druid, the house of the wedding, the trap-door, the hamlet, the trees, the hill, the Rhine and its banks, the heaven and the stars, all disappeared at the same moment, and I awoke in my arm-chair, surrounded by my poor books, which had just fallen from my knees.

The dinner bell was still ringing.

IV.

IV.

You may rest assured, I did not merely dream of that bold transformation of Teutons into Titans ; one of the most learned and most reliable authors in my library, assures me of the fact. These great scholars are sometimes very clever men.

According to this authority, the Celts were very much taller than the Greeks, and this fact had naturally suggested to the latter the idea of speaking of them as giants. The Celtic Pelasgi, who were warlike shepherds like all the men of their race, usually watched their flocks as they were grazing on the high mountains, and it was these mountains which the myth accused them of piling up, one upon another, to scale the heavens. You will say, What mad follies of poets! I grant this; but after these mad poets came men like Hesiod and Homer, who changed the idle dream into stern reality, and upon this rock a new religion was founded, and with it, a new civilization.

Now the day has come when these same gods of Greece, having become the gods of great Rome, will pursue the Titans, or Teutons, to the very heart of Germany.

It is well known that Cæsar, after having conquered Gaul, had promptly crossed the Rhine, rather for the purpose of making a reconnaissance on the opposite bank of the river, than with any view to conquest. His successor went farther into Germany. Drusus, the adopted son of Augustus, and his lieutenant, reached the banks of the river Elbe, pursuing the Franks, the Teutons, the Burgundians, the Cheruski, the Marcomanni, all those children of the same great family, who had been overcome, put to flight, but never subjugated. All of a sudden, at the very moment when he is about to cross the river, there comes forth from the dark, dense forest, not a new army of barbarians, bristling with spears and halberts, but a woman, a tall, haughty looking woman, with long disheveled hair

A DRUIDESS ENDOWED WITH THE GIFT OF PROPHECY.

THE VICTORIOUS MARCH OF THE ROMANS.

flowing down upon her bare shoulders, and on her brow a crown of simple oak branches.

She steps across his path and with uplifted finger orders him in an imperious voice to turn back and to go to his camp to prepare for death.

It was a Druidess, endowed in the highest degree with the gift of prophecy; so it would seem at least, for Drusus had hardly entered the Roman camp, when he fell from his horse and expired.

Not all the Druidesses, however, succeeded in making the Roman generals go back, by a word or a gesture; nor did all the Roman generals fall from their horses and die. After fifty-five years of strangely varying fortunes, the Genius of Rome was victorious, and must needs have been victorious, for it led the whole world by its power. It brought with it also its gods, which in spite of their numbers, or rather perhaps because they were so numerous, met on the banks of the Rhine with a more determined resistance than its soldiers.

Rome had a magnificent mission to fulfill. Her glorious duty upon earth was to restore the unity of all the great human families, and to improve their condition by bringing them in contact with each other — by fraternity, in fine. To attain this end, she had generally employed War as her principal instrument; Religion had been a subsidiary agent only, a weapon which she kept concealed, but which she used with great efficacy to secure the permanency of her conquests.

Unfortunately, Roman gods were as liable to corruption, and to fearful corruption, as the great men of the Empire. Nations rise step by step on the grand ladder of civilization; when they have reached the top they must keep up their activity, without which no life and no progress can be maintained, and thus the moment comes when they are forced to descend again, till at last they sink into sensual degradation, into erudite, refined, voluptuous barbarism — the very bottom of the ladder.

Rome had begun by raising altars to all the virtues; now her deities personified nothing but vices. How could they expect to introduce them

and make them acceptable to these coarse Germans, among whom prostitution, adultery, and theft were hardly known by name, who allowed a woman to claim hospitality at the house of any *Karl*, to rest under his roof, and even to share his couch, without fearing slander, if he had but put a naked sword between her and himself, and who had never known and could not know the use of locks and keys? Were they not accustomed to hang their most valuable possessions upon the branches of a consecrated tree in the open camp, or to place them on top of a druidical stone or beneath it, as they chose — knowing that there they were perfectly safe? When they had taken this simple precaution, they could go to bed and sleep quietly, and there was no need for putting a sentinel on guard.

Already, in the days of Cæsar, the Romans had employed a very ingenious and cunning device, in order to win over the simple Gauls. They had pretended to find their gods, their own peculiar gods, already established in the country from olden times. Thus there existed in Gaul a statue which the Etrusci had erected in honor of *Ogmius*, or rather *Ogma*. The Greek Lucian mentions it in these words: —

"It is a decrepit old man; his skin is black; this form of a man, however, wears the attributes of Hercules, the lion's skin and the club.

"I thought at first," Lucian adds, "that the Celts had invented this odd figure in order to laugh at

7

the gods of Greece; but this so-called Hercules, who is of very great antiquity, drags after him a multitude of men, whom he leads by golden chains which he holds in his mouth, while they are fastened to the ears of his victims."

This *Ogmius* was evidently a typical representation of Druidism itself; *Ogma*, in Celtic languages, means both science and eloquence. What has Hercules to do with all this? Nevertheless the Romans insisted upon calling him by that name.

Nor did they stop here.

When they found all the nations they had conquered were continually speaking of a certain *Teutates*, they at once declared that they recognized in
this popular person their own god Mercury. It was
he and no other! It was Mercury, the son of Jupiter and the nymph Maïa. There was a striking
resemblance, an unmistakable analogy! No one
could misapprehend the thing for an instant!

Oh, my good Romans, I don't mean to blame you
now for all the trouble you gave me when I was at
college! I will forget all that — But what could
make you conceive this stupid idea, of naturalizing
among us your Mercury, the god of eloquence, if

you choose, but above all the ever ready pimp of
Jupiter, the god of trade and of thieves, and of
naturalizing him in a land where trade, love, and
thieves are so little known! In subservience to this
Roman notion, some of our modern writers have
been clever enough to prove that there were really
many points of resemblance between Mercury and
Teutates — but I, I openly deny it! Once more,
philology shall come to my assistance, to overturn
their doctrine. It was only this morning, while
shaving, that I made a philologic discovery of the
very highest importance, in which the public will
take the most lively interest, and, I doubt not, the
French Acadamy also.

The word *Teut*, as the reader no doubt knows
perfectly well, means *God; Tat* in ancient Celtic
and in modern Breton may be accurately rendered
as *father* — so an old Breton woman assures me,
who brought me up when I was a child. Add to
Tat the termination *Es*, the diminutive form of
Esus, the *Lord*, connect the three monosyllables,
and you have *Teut-Tat-Es*, God, Father, and Lord!

Where — I appeal to all the famous historians so
graphically described by Rabelais — where do you
find a trace of Mercury in Teutates now? He is
beyond all doubt the great divinity of the Celts,
but you found it more convenient to follow the
interested views of the Roman writers. And yet

even if they were innocent of any design upon your
credulity, might they not have been mistaken themselves? Are you not aware that Plutarch, conscientious Plutarch himself, after having witnessed the
Feast of Tabernacles in Palestine, tells us gravely
that the Jews worshipped Bacchus? You were not
aware of it, come, confess it frankly! For I will confess to you, that I was not aware of it, myself, ten
minutes ago; but Dr. Rosahl has just told me so.
The good doctor is delighted at my discovery of the
true meaning of *Teut-Tat-Es ;* he thinks no etymo-
logical question of such importance was ever more
satisfactorily put and answered in the same breath.
He advises me strongly to write a memoir on the
subject, which he will undertake to bring to the
notice of learned societies, and only suggests the
expediency of leaving out any allusion to my old
Breton nurse ; but I am too conscientious a writer
ever to omit quoting my authorities.

Now, since I have mentioned Rabelais, let us
" return to our lambs," that is, to our Teutons.

After the Roman conquest, the same transformation of native deities into classic gods continued in
Germany. The sacred oak was changed into Jupiter, whom it represented symbolically; the Druidical altars became either Apollo or Diana; sometimes they were made to represent deities of inferior
rank, nymphs, anything in fact. But these numer-

ous metamorphoses, made rather hastily, led to a curious mistake.

The conquerors had met on the banks of the Weser a huge monolith, cut with an axe by simple and ignorant stone-carvers. It was called *Irmensul.* Like the Celtic Teutates, this Irmensul also attracted at certain fixed times an immense concourse of people. The Romans, appreciating the martial spirit of the natives, did not hesitate to declare that this was Mars, their god of war. Thereupon they paid it all possible honor, consecrating their weapons to the new deity, and offering countless propitiatory sacrifices.

Now, who was this Irmensul?

When Varus had invaded Germany, during the reign of Augustus, at the head of three legions, Arminius, a chieftain of the Cheruski (a Brunswicker, we would say nowadays), had surprised him, and completely surrounded his army in the marshes of Teutoburg, on the banks of the Weser. Every man of this army, whether a Roman or a warrior of the allied tribes wearing Roman livery, had perished by the sword. For eight days the bloody waters of the Weser had carried down more than thirty thousand dead bodies.

When the news of this disaster reached Augustus, he thought that Gaul was lost, Italy in danger, and Rome herself imperilled. Mad with grief, he would rise, for a month afterwards, night after night, and in his terror wander through his vast palace, crying out: "O Varus, Varus, bring me back my legions!"

Well, the Irmensul was nothing more than a triumphal column erected in honor of Arminius and his Cheruski. *Irmen* is the same as the name *Herman* or *Armin* (Arminius), and *sul* means column. The Romans, however, did not know this, and they paid dearly for their ignorance. If they had known better they would not have committed the egregious blunder of kneeling down and worshipping the man who had destroyed the three legions of Varus. It is very evident that they were as ignorant of German as of Celtic.

It ought not to surprise us, however, to see the
soldiers of the imperial people change stones into
gods, as Deucalion had changed them into men.
Before the days of Homer, and for a long time
after him, Jupiter was in Seleucia modestly represented by a fragment of rock and Cybele by a
black stone. In Cyprus, the Venus of Paphos was
nothing but a triangular or quadrangular pyramid,
nor can I imagine what importance could be attached to three or four angles in a body, which
was soon to assume the softest and most fascinat-
ing outlines. First the poets had come and sung
of Cybele, the kind goddess, of Jupiter the omnipotent, and of Venus, the soul of the world and the
queen of beauty. Inspired by their voice and the
bold conceptions of their fancy, the sculptors had
next employed the chisel upon these stones and
these pyramids, and there had sprung forth from
these shapeless masses the Lord of Gods, armed
with his lightning, the beautiful Cytherea, armed
with the most powerful weapons of all womanly
graces. Oh, poets and sculptors, you have upset
everything in religion ! You are responsible for
the loss of that austere simplicity which once char-
acterized the faith of men ! Miserable cutters of
stone, reckless counters of syllables, you, and you
alone, have substituted symbols for truth ! Still, I
do not condemn you; although I have stood up to

defend the Druids of the earliest days, I am far from being insensible to the charms of art and of poetry; besides, what right have I, who speak of gods and myths, to pass sentence on those who have been the real creators of Mythology?

While the conquerors of the Teutons, in the

pride of their cleverness, were committing blunder after blunder, and fell into the pits they had dug for others, the real gods of Rome stayed on the banks of the Rhine, where they had already been accepted by the Gauls. They were impatient enough to see Germany also erect them temples and statues, but the Rhine with uplifted waves barred the passage.

Perhaps the old river remembered his grievances

of former days, when he had been compelled to
appear in the triumphal processions of Germanicus,
as a conquered river, loaded with chains, while the
rabble and riffraff of Rome had insulted him to his
face and covered him from head to foot with the
mud of the Tiber.

The remembrance of his former humiliation
seemed to revive his wrath at this day, and he
unfolded his whole strength to take his revenge.
In vain had the Olympians tried repeatedly to cross
at different points; everywhere, from the Alps to
the Northern Sea, they found him furious, roaring
and rushing, full of threats in his green waters and
besprinkling the banks with white foam.

At last they bribed him to espouse the cause of

the Empire: they made
him a king, the king of
German rivers. A king
more or less mattered
very little to a people
who made and unmade
kings at will.

The Rhine was evi-
dently flattered by the
distinction; and he laid
aside his long cherished
wrath.

He had already allowed Jupiter to cross, taking

him perhaps for Esus; he now carefully examined
the passports and certificates of good conduct of
several other gods, and left the way open for Apollo

and Minerva, Diana and some deities of fair re-
pute; but when he saw Bacchus, his anger was
rekindled. What? Were not the Germans mad
and quarrelsome enough, when they had only
taken too much beer? How could he consent to
allow their passions to be aroused by potent wine?
He was king, and as such bound to keep this
scourge from his people.

The gods whom he had allowed to cross endeavored to plead for the son of Semele, — but he
remained inexorable. His severity relaxed, however,
when the vines planted by order of the Emperor

Probus in parts of the Rheingau, began to adorn
the banks of the river with their verdure — he was

overcome, when he had once tasted the juice of
the grape.   He consented to let Bacchus pass
from bank to bank, but only at the time of the
vintage.

Once admitted, Bacchus soon brought into the
land the whole crowd of gods and goddesses, who
made up his following and who enjoyed no great
reputation in Rome and in Greece.   The Rhine

became angry once more, but once more caresses and unexpected honors had their hoped-for effect. He was already a king; he now became a god.

Henceforth Father Rhine conceived a strong

affection for his former adversaries. When he saw that the German bank had adopted the customs and the religion of the conquerors as fully as the Celtic bank, he abandoned completely his restrictive policy and did his best to help everybody across. Thus Jupiter was no sooner installed in Germany, than he summoned his Corybantes ; Bacchus his Bacchantes and his Mænads, Diana

her hunting nymphs, Venus her whole court of
lascivious priestesses; the Dryads and the Hama-

dryads, the Naiads and the Tritons, the Fauns and
the Silvans, all came one by one. It was a perfect invasion.

Germany, grave and solemn as she was, felt not
a little troubled by this wholesale irruption of friv-

olous and ill-mannered deities, who so little agreed
with her austere habits. The young, it is true, were
more easily Romanized and readily caught at this
poetical personification of all the forces of Nature;
but the old, the chieftains, and above all the Druids,
backed by a nearly unanimous people, asked each
other what could be the meaning of this sudden
enthusiasm for new gods, this half mad devotion
to celestial clowns?

No one, however, dared to raise a hand; the
Teutons had lost their former energy, they were
enfeebled, unnerved and exhausted by their long
but useless resistance. Hence, like true cowards,
they appeared in the pagan temples, in order to
conciliate the good-will of the conquerors, and then,
to pacify their consciences, they hastened to some
dark forest and there with anxious eyes and disturbed minds, they offered in fear and trembling
their fervent worship to the sacred oak.

The Roman gods were soon to encounter far
more formidable adversaries elsewhere.

Far beyond Germany, as we find it described
and limited by geographers, there lived a host of
nations, scattered over a vast territory, and extend-
ing as far East as the shores of the Caspian Sea.
The Romans had never penetrated far into these
unknown depths, which sent forth incessantly new
armies of soldiers whom they classed indiscrim-

inately under the vague and collective name of
Hyperboreans. Such were the Huns, the Scythians,
the Goths, the Slaves (Poles, **Danes**, Swedes,
Russians, and Norwegians), all of them robbers and
pirates. Some, under the name of Cimbrians, had
joined the Teutons and with them invaded Gaul
and even Italy, till they encountered the armies of
Marius ; others, were about to cross the Pyrenees
and to fall upon Spain. Among them all, the
Scandinavians were by far the most powerful, intrepid soldiers and fearless sailors, who were soon
to darken the waters of the Rhine with their countless vessels, and to make Charlemagne shed tears
as he thought of the days to come.

Ere long these dauntless pirates will actually enter
the Loire, then even the Seine; they will besiege
Paris, and finally, thanks to the able statesmanship
of King Charles, whom they call the Simple, they
will become. Christians, after a fashion, and under
the name of Normans take possession of one of
the fairest provinces of France. Then they will
cultivate the soil which they had heretofore robbed
of its produce, they will drink beer instead of
cider, they will peacefully devote themselves to
lawsuits and cattle-raising, and will end by wearing
white cotton night-caps — after having destroyed
Rome and conquered England twice.

The Scandinavians, of Celtic origin like the

Gauls and the Germans, led at first both nomadic and sedentary lives and were rather barbarous than unpolished; but they built cities and erected temples, in which they worshipped Odin the One-Eyed.

If the harvest failed, or whenever the first warmth of spring aroused in them their innate fondness of vagabondage and war, they took to their boats or mounted their horses, and the stupefied nations

8

of Europe watched the horizon and listened along
the river courses, to distinguish whether this great
Northern tempest, this storm of iron and fire, of
blood and of tears, was rushing down upon them
by land or by sea.

After having crossed Germany in all directions,
some of these bands, or rather some remnants of
such bands, settled from inclination or from necessity, in certain portions of the country, especially
on the islands in the Main, the Weser, and the
Neckar. Their priests soon made numerous converts among the neighbors to the faith of Odin.
The Germans paid little heed to the difference between Odin and Teut. . The two names designated,
for them, one and the same god, the one god of
the Celts.

The increasing influence of these Druids of the
third epoch led, however, naturally to some opposition. The German priests accused them of being
too profuse in the shedding of blood, and of having
given their god Odin a companion in a certain
god Thor, fond of overcoming giants, and of having thus destroyed the true nature of the original
creed, which knew but one God.

A schism was about to divide the Druidical
church, when the arrival of the Roman deities
brought the two opposite parties once more together. Each yielded somewhat ; they came to an

THE GREAT NORTHERN TEMPEST.

understanding and finally joined hands in a con-
spiracy. The Scandinavian Druids, forsaking the
prudent reserve which they had so far scrupulously
observed, declared that, in order to triumph over the
Roman Olympians, Odin had not only the assistance of his all-powerful son Thor, but could, if he
chose, summon an escort of gods at least as imposing in numbers as that of Jupiter himself.

The German Druids veiled their faces, but the
people and the whole party which was opposed to
Jupiter the wicked, and to Venus the shameless,
joyfully accepted the proposition. However cruel
the Scandinavian ritual appeared with its increased
number of victims who had to be offered to the
new gods, it seemed to them better still to worship Terror than to worship disgraceful Voluptu-
ousness. They acknowledged Odin and his son
Thor, and impatiently waited for the arrival of the
others.

The German Druids gave way, hoping perhaps
that the two hosts of deities would erelong fall out
among themselves and soon destroy each other.

Father Rhine, in his equal affection for all his
brother gods, was far too good-natured to take this
admission of new deities amiss, and promptly went
northward, to the most hyperborean regions of snow
and ice, in search of the newly chosen gods.

The two parties soon met face to face.

It is our solemn duty to explain fully the whole curious system of Scandinavian gods. We shall see that here, as in all that we shall have to add, legends, myths, and traditions abound in such numbers that they can be had for the asking.

V.

V.

THE world was not born.

Thick mists, unbroken by light, unbounded in limit, filled space.

After a long period of darkness, silence, and perfect repose, a faint light is seen, vague and uncertain, hardly deserving the name ; something is moving unsteadily in this night. The giant Ymer has been born spontaneously out of the mixture and assimilation of these closely compressed mists, which sudden and severe frost has condensated.

At that time men of science had not yet discussed the question of spontaneous generation; not one academy made mention of the subject.

Ymer, the sole inhabitant, the Robinson Crusoe of this world of darkness, became tired of his solitude. Guessing how he had been born himself, he gathered the mists that surrounded him, piled them one upon the other, shaped them into a form resembling his own, and once more the North wind came and solidified the mists. As he was a giant, he created giants; he also created mountains, no doubt for the purpose of furnishing seats for these giants, for the highest among them did not reach up to their belts. This does not mean, that these mountains were less high than they are nowadays, but the sons of Ymer were of such size that without bending down a little, they could not have rested their elbows on the summit of Chimborazo, and what is more marvelous still, Ymer himself not only was taller than every one of his sons, but taller than all of his sons together, standing one upon the shoulders of the other! When he stretched himself out full length, the Alps might have served him as a pillow, while his feet would have rested on Mount Caucasus.

THE GIANT YMER HAS BEEN BORN.

In order to produce such giants and such mountains, he had, of course, to consume large quantities
of the material furnished by the chaos of mists;
the remainder of this gaseous substance, trembling
in vacant space and losing its balance, fell back
into the depths of the valleys, and formed the
ocean.

Some few animals began soon to stir in the
waters, and on the shores of that vast sea; sphinxes
and dragons, hydras and griffins, kraken and levia-
thans, all creatures of a low order, but in their
proportions adapted to this colossal world, this
world of the infinitely great, and no doubt related
in some manner to the antediluvian families of
mammoths and pterodactyls, of ichthyosauri and
plesiosauri.

A god of the first race, a creator without being
created, Ymer naturally did not possess that skill
and that cleverness which can only be acquired by
long experience. However strange, therefore, it
may appear, however inexplicable, the fact is, that
this world, fresh with new life and freed from the
original mists, was nevertheless covered with darkness. The only light which existed was an occa-
sional phosphorescence of the sea or a few flashes
of electric light, such as an aurora borealis
sends forth; and this faint glimmer alone illumined
the pathway of those vast creatures, those mon-

strous reptiles, who, dazzled for an instant, plunged back into the lowest depths of the waters, casting up huge waves and tall columns of spray.

It must have been a peculiarly curious sight, certainly, to see those Giants of the Frost, as they were called, wandering through the darkness across the boundless plains and along endless shores, under a sky without light, looking for each other from one end of the world to the other. To be sure, they could accomplish the journey in a few long strides, and if they were peculiarly anxious to see each other, face to face, they had only to wait for the chance of a momentary flash or a faint twilight glimmer.

The sight was no doubt curious, but there was no one to behold it.

This state of things could not last long. With a new god a new world also came into existence. This new god was very different from the first, it was Light itself, condensed at the southern extremity of the heavens, far from this earth inhabited by giants.

One fine day — an unlucky day for them, however — these giants noticed that the sky above their heads was suddenly assuming a faint pinkish hue, then violet, and finally purple. At this they rejoiced. But suddenly a ball of fire appeared, and they were terrified. It was Odin, Odin followed by his celestial family, which consisted at least of a dozen principal deities!

But no! no! I take it back! I rebel! No one can come in contact with these ancient myths, without knocking against some principle of astronomy. Astronomers find only seven principal deities in Scandinavian mythology, when they are called upon to transform them into planets, and twelve, when the question is about the signs of the Zodiac. That seems to me to make mythology a little too easy. Does it not look as if the first men had been born with a telescope and a compass in their pocket, and as if they had erected an observatory long before they thought of building huts for themselves?

Fortunately I am not bound to follow their footsteps.

Certain historians of high authority have found out that Odin lived upon earth before he came to dwell in heaven. He was an illustrious conqueror,

very expert at killing men, one of those scourges
of God, who fall upon nations in order to break
them to pieces. As a matter of course, these nations deified him after his death.

I see nothing astronomical in all this.

Hence, I return to my own method, and propose to describe him, as he appeared to his Druids,
his Scalds, and his worshippers.

"YMER WAS THE FIRST TO SUCCUMB." (p. 131.)

He arrived from the southern countries, no doubt
from the Orient, bringing with him the sun, as an
indispensable auxiliary in the great task which

"AFTER THE GIANTS CAME THE TURN OF LAND AND SEA MONSTERS." (p. 131.)

9

he had undertaken, to reform this dark and ice-covered world: "For there was a time," says the Edda, the bible of the Scandinavians, "when the sun, the moon, and the stars did not know the place they were to occupy. It was then the gods assembled and agreed as to the post which was to be assigned to each one of them."

When the installation of the heavenly bodies had thus been agreed upon, Odin followed the example of all the Hercules of Egypt and of Greece, and began his benevolent career by freeing the earth of all the monsters by which it was infested. Ymer was the first to succumb to his blows, and after him, the other giants of the frost, "a race of evil-doers," adds the Edda. Evildoers? Whom did they aggrieve, I wonder? The complainants must have been the kraken, the griffins, and the serpents.

The world had hardly come into existence and already the right of the stronger had established the doctrine: *Væ victis !*

Of all the giants of the frost a single one escaped. He must have been a married man, for his descendants became after a while so numerous as to trouble the Ases, that is to say, Odin and his companions, the other gods.

After the giants, came the turn of land and sea monsters, who were almost as formidable as they themselves. In the general destruction two mon-

sters only survived : the wolf Fenris, with his fearful jaws, which enabled him to crush mountains
and even to injure the sun, and the serpent Iormungandur, the great sea serpent of world-wide
renown. Both these monsters were one day to
aid the giants of the frost in avenging themselves
on their conqueror.

Odin thought he had now nothing more to fear,

and returned to the realms of light, there to enjoy
his glory in peace and to revel in the delights of
Walhalla.

One morning he came down to see how the world was coming on since he had reorganized it, and he found to his great joy, that the new creation was assuming a more pleasing appearance. Grass was growing in the plains, on the slopes of hills, and even at the bottom of the rivers and the sea; here and there trees of varied forms and shapes arose and gave variety to the monotonous horizon; some, crowding together in groups on the mountain side, seemed to whisper confidentially to each other, as the breeze was lightly agitating their foliage, while others stood together in countless hosts, stretching away over hill and dale as far as eye could reach, but silent and immovable, like an army which remains motionless, while the chiefs are deliberating.

Behind the green curtain of forests, deer, eland,

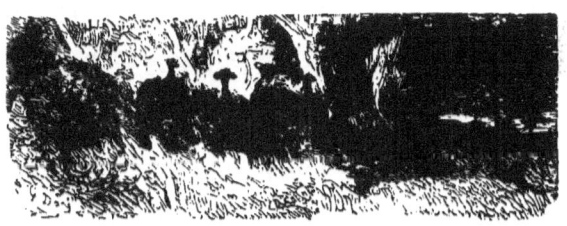

and aurochs were bounding in herds, now and then showing their beautiful horns or their dark bushy brows at the opening of some clearing; goats were climbing about on the rocks and venturing close to the brink of precipices ; birds were singing in the groves, now swinging playfully on the supple branches of willows, and now darting suddenly on swift wings through the air ; fish were gliding silently under the surface of the waters, which reflected their silvery sheen or broke in soft ripples, while butterflies and insects were sporting and buzzing around beautiful flowers.

Odin smiled ; the artist was pleased with his work.

But were animals, impelled by natural instincts only and exclusively occupied with the desire to satisfy their coarse wants, were such animals worthy to be the sole owners of such a charming abode ?

It occurred to him to invent a being which, without participating in the divine essence, might still rise high above all other creatures. This time the divine artist wanted a spectator, to witness his work, to appreciate it intelligently, and afterwards to profit by it for some good purpose.

He was meditating on it during a walk on the sea-shore, when a piece of wood, a fragment of a huge branch of a tree which the wind had broken off, attracted his attention. It had evidently fallen into a river, which had carried it out into the high sea, and there it had been beaten and bruised by ebb and tide. He drew this poor shapeless stick of wood towards him, split it in two and made out of it a man and a woman.

" Do you hear? Do you understand ? " Asks the Edda, at this point.

Now, what is this intended to convey to us ? That man, exposed to the caprices of the elements, is nothing but a poor plaything in the hands of Fate? Very well, let us admit this explanation. But can the sacred book of the Scandinavians really presume to teach us that the origin of man- kind must be looked for in two sticks of wood? We cannot but think that that would be a sorry jest, alike unworthy of the general solemnity of the Edda and of the mysterious majesty of ancient cosmogonies.

Besides, we ought not to forget that all the Northern nations attributed a divine character to trees; if in Germany the oak was held sacred, the hyperboreans held the ash tree in great respect, and the question is only whether our first father was made of the wood of an ash tree, an oak, or a willow.

This leads us naturally to the consideration of the ash *Ygdrasil* and its curious population of gods, birds, and quadrupeds.

The branches of this marvelous tree spread over the whole surface of the earth; its top supported the Walhalla and rose to the uppermost heavens, while its roots penetrated to the very bottom of hell. Under its shadow dwell Odin and his Ases, when the government of the world requires his presence, or some important question has to be decided.

Two swift winged ravens are incessantly flying to and fro in the Universe, to see what is going on; then they come and perch, one on his left and one on his right shoulder, and whisper into his ear the news of the day. A squirrel, as swift in its movements as the two ravens, is perpetually running up and down the tree. If you doubt my word, hear what the poet says: —

. . . . The fearful Odin
Was seated beneath the ancient ash,
The sacred tree whose immortal brow
Rises and touches the vault of heaven.

On the top an eagle with eager eyes,
With piercing eyes, with ever open eyes,
Takes in the whole Universe in a single glance.
Odin receives his swift messages.
Incessantly a tiny squirrel
Comes and goes ; the god's voice cheers it onward.
All at once it dashes from the trunk to the top
And in an instant it returns again
From the top to the trunk. Odin, when it comes,
'Turns an attentive ear to the squirrel. . . . .

But the poet does not tell the whole story. To act as a check upon the reports of the eagle, the ravens, and the squirrel, a vulture is perching

upon the loftiest top of the sacred tree, who looks
over all the horizons of the earth and the universe,
watching for the slightest stir and giving notice of
any important event by his cries or the flapping of
his wings.

Still other animals, however, inhabit the great
ash tree Ygdrasil. Some of these play a sinister
part in the great menagerie; they are hideous reptiles, half concealed in the slimy marshes into which
one of the roots of the tree finds its way, and ever
striving to pour their venom into the mire; beneath another root a dragon is crouching, who constantly gnaws at it, and four starving deer, rushing
through its branches, forever devour its foliage.

"Do you hear? Do you understand?" asks the
Edda once more.

For the present we do not presume to interpret
these descriptions, and before we attempt to pene-
trate into these dark mysteries, we will mention
the principal chiefs among the Ases.

The mystic marriage of Odin and Frigg resulted
in the god Thor, who is held in equal veneration
with his father. As his duty is to carry thunder
and lightning, it is he who shakes the earth whenever he drives through the clouds in his car drawn
by two goats and producing a noise represented by
the words : " *Pumerle pump ! Pumerle pump !
Pliz ! Pluz ! Schmi ! Schmur ! Tarantara ! Tarantara !* "

This onomatopoetic translation of the flashing of lightning and the rolling of thunder, is not my own; it comes directly from Dr. Martin Luther, the great Reformer.

Thor is also engaged in pursuing and destroying the giants of the mountains, degenerate children of the giants of the frost, in size at least. At a later period we shall meet with giants of still smaller dimensions. Alas! that here below everything that is great and strong has a tendency to decrease steadily!

For this war against the giants Odin has bestowed upon his son three precious objects, which in the inventory of the Ases appear under the name of *Thor's Three Jewels*. The first is his weighty hammer, *Mjöiner* (some people call it his club), which goes forth by itself to meet giants and crushes their heads. One of the commentators upon the  Edda professes to see in the giants of the mountains nothing but the mountains themselves, and in the hammer Mjöiner, nothing but lightning, which generally strikes their summit. We must evidently put as little faith in commentators as in astronomers.

The second of Thor's jewels was a pair of iron gloves. As soon as he puts them on, his spear no sooner reaches the point at which it is aimed, than it returns to his hand, precisely as the falcon comes back to the keeper's gauntlet, after having destroyed its victim.

The third jewel of Thor is his war belt; when he puts it on, his strength is twice as great as before; in fact, he becomes irresistible and would overthrow the great Odin himself. But Odin has nothing to fear on his part, for in spite of his brutal and passionate temper, Thor is always an obedient and submissive son.

Asa-Thor, that is to say, the Lord Thor, was most highly respected among men as the red-haired master of thunder and lightning, and as the destroyer of giants; and he was also greatly feared as an active, blustering god, of a troublesome, turbulent temper and of somewhat eccentric manners.

Another weapon, at least as marvelous as Asa-Thor's famous hammer, was the sword of the god Freyr. This sword was endowed with an intelligence very rarely to be met with among swords, and punctually obeyed the orders of its master. Even in his absence, it went promptly and faithfully to carry out his orders, striking here and there at a given point, or making terrible havoc in the midst of a battle, without a hand at the hilt to direct its mortal blows.

The good Freyr, as pacific a god as ever lived, was quite indifferent to battles and fights; hence he gave his orders quietly to his faithful sword, while he remained comfortably seated at Odin's table, enjoying his strong beer and the rarest wines.

I cannot help wishing that they might have known the art of manufacturing guns after this system, at the time when I was a lieutenant in the Belleville National Guard. It would have been so pleasant to see a rifle move gravely to and fro, quite alone, in front of the City Hall and the Guard House; or to meet a patrol of four guns, accompanied by a corporal, but a flesh and blood corporal to cry out: Who is there? In the meantime the happy owners of these improved

FREYR.

weapons might have been sitting, not at Odin's table, but at the nearest coffee house or restaurant, drinking beer or wine just like the Scandinavian gods.

Unfortunately our manufacturers of arms have not yet reached that degree of skill, which our forefathers seem to have possessed, and thus I have never yet been able to enjoy such a sight.

The happy owner of this magic weapon, Freyr, presided over the general administration of the clouds; it was he who made fine weather or rain, a very troublesome office, which must have exposed him to countless petitions and most contradictory prayers.

His sister Freya, afterwards called Frigg, was Odin's wife and the most honored goddess on earth as well as in heaven. She inspired and pro-tected lovers, and very different from her sister in Greece, this Northern Venus enjoyed an unsullied reputation.

They say that once, when her husband had gone away on a long journey, she was so deeply grieved at his absence, that her tears ran day and night incessantly; these tears, however, differed from those of mortal beings; they were all drops of gold which fell into her bosom, and hence the Northern people call the precious metal to this day *Freya's tears.*

One only among all the dwellers in Walhalla had been able to give her some comfort by singing

his sweetest songs ; this was the god Bragi, the
god of poetry and beautiful words.

A tradition which deserves to be mentioned here,
accounts for the manner in which he obtained this
precious gift of eloquence and the art of poetry.

In the early days of the world, when the creating god had concentrated, so to say, all the active
powers of humanity in a few individuals, and when
a long life permitted these favored beings to carry
on their studies till they reached a happy end,
there lived on earth a wise man who possessed an
art unknown, not among men only, but among the
gods themselves. This was the art of perpetuating
thoughts by word-painting, of reproducing them in
outward forms, not to the eye by colors, but to the
ear by sounds. This sage was called Kvasir. He
had invented the *Runes*, the art of poetry, and the
no less precious art of reproducing words and fixing
them in writing. He cut his runes on beech tablets; if he had gone a step farther, he would have
invented printing long before Guttenberg.

Kvasir was then the sole owner of the art of
Poetry.

Two wicked dwarfs prowling about in search of
treasures, took it into their heads, that the treasure
of Poetry was better than any other, and forthwith
determined to obtain possession of it. They killed
Kvasir, into whose dwelling they had crept by

stealth, and as they were masters in magic, like all the dwarfs of those days, they carefully collected his blood, and mixing it, in different proportions, with honey, put it into three vessels, which they closed hermetically. These three vessels contained respectively Logic, Eloquence, and Poetry. To keep them safe till the day on which they should be used, they buried them in the depths of a cave which was inaccessible to men and unknown to the gods themselves. But one of those travelling agents, who under the form of ravens, were continually wandering over the world in Odin's employ, had been a silent witness of the transactions, the murder, the mixing, and the hiding of the three vessels. He returned instantly to the ash Ygdrasil and reported it all to his master. The god gave his orders, which the squirrel, no doubt, at once carried to the eagle, and the latter, who was continually on the watch on the top of the sacred tree, left his post for a few moments in charge of the vulture, and flew with rapid wings to the cave, from whence he returned laden with the three precious vessels. It is to be supposed that he carried one in his beak, and the two others, one in each of his claws.

He placed the mysterious vessels at Odin's feet and at once returned to relieve the vulture and to resume his watch.

Odin opened first the vessel which contained

10

Poetry and tasted the contents. From that moment
he never spoke otherwise than in verse. He also
tasted Logic, and henceforth he spoke and reasoned
with such extreme accuracy, that he found no one
to agree with him any longer ; he tasted Eloquence,
and as soon as he opened his lips, he might have
been mistaken for one of our own most eminent
lawyers. Gold chains seemed to come out from
his lips, as was the case with Ogmius, with which
he bound the ears and hearts of all his hearers.

Whilst he was thus enjoying himself, Bragi his
son, and Saga his daughter, who were sitting by
him, felt their mouths water and looked imploringly
at him.

Setting aside the terror with which the Druids
have surrounded Odin, he seems to have been
occasionally good-natured, and certainly always acted
like a kind father. He offered the vessel with
Poetry first to Saga, courteously giving her the
preference on account of her sex. She barely
touched it with her lips. When Bragi's turn came,
he eagerly swallowed as much as he could, and
without taking time to gather breath, he began a
grand triumphal chant in honor of the feasts, the
loves, the wars, and the greatness of the gods, the
stars of the firmament, paradise, hell, and the ash
Ygdrasil. In well chosen cadences he imitated the
clanking of cups, the cooing of doves and of lovers,

BRAGI AND THE BEAUTIFUL FREYA.

the tumult of battles, the harmonies of the celestial spheres, and all this with such energy, such fire and such grace by turns, that Odin was enchanted, and having become a master himself about five minutes ago, on the spot changed his name of the Long-bearded God, which he had borne so far, to that of the God of Poetry. Moreover, he entrusted to his keeping the threefold treasure which had been taken from Kvasir's murderers.

This was that god Bragi who alone succeeded in comforting the beautiful and inconsolable Freya in her great grief.

Through him the Druids were instructed in the art of verse; to him is due that terrible Scandinavian poetry, which contains, according to Ozanam, quite as much blood as honey.

As to Saga, she became the goddess of Tradition. " The heart of history is in tradition," says a master, a sage, and a poet.

Good goddess Saga, your lips, I know, never touched the vessel containing Eloquence, nor that which held Logic, far from it! And still I count upon you to support me in carrying out my work, which I have perhaps imprudently begun ; for I begin to be overwhelmed with materials, the subject is a very grave one, and, in spite of the good advice of my learned doctor and the assistance of my two charming lady-companions, time and strength threaten not to suffice. Therefore I beseech you, as well as my readers, to grant me a short repose, before I proceed any farther on my journey through Odin's fantastic world.

VI.   -

VI.

WE have no intention of giving here a complete list of the numerous deities of the North. We will

only mention Hermode, Odin's messenger and man
of business; Forseti, the peacemaker; Widar, the
god of silence, a dumb person who only walks on
air, as if he were afraid to hear the noise of his
own footsteps; Vali, the skilfull archer; Uller, the
excellent skater, who taught the giant Tialff his
art, in spite of what the poet Klopstock says to
the contrary; Hoder, a mysterious deity, whose
name must never be uttered by any one in heaven
or on earth. Why not? Odin alone knows the
reason.

Let us also mention Heimdall, with the golden
teeth. A son of Odin, he had nine mothers —
eight more than had ever been known before him.
He is the guardian of Walhalla, and his duty is to
watch lest the giants should one fine day attempt
to storm the heavenly abode by means of the
Bifrost bridge, that is, the rainbow. But the gods
can sleep in peace; neither the eagle nor the
ravens on the ash Ygdrasil can surpass Heimdall in
vigilance. The senses of sight and hearing are in
him developed to a perfectly marvelous degree;
he can hear the grass grow in the meadows and
the wool grow on the back of the sheep. From
one end of the world he sees a fly pass through
the air at the other end, and, more than that, he
sees distinctly the different joints in its feet and
the black or brown spots with which its wings are

dotted. In the midst of the darkest night and at the bottom of the sea where it is deepest, he sees an atom moving and watches the marriage of monads. There is nothing in the whole universe hid from him.

But why should this god Heimdall have golden teeth, after a fashion of some of the natives of Sunda? Odin alone knows the reason.

Among all these gods Balder is the most richly endowed, the best, the handsomest and the most virtuous — Balder, the Bright God, by eminence. Although the son of Odin and Frigg, he might be taken for a son of Freya, on account of his strong resemblance to Love itself, not to the turbulent, passionate, and capricious Love of the Greeks, but to Love in the widest and noblest sense of the word, — Love, in fine, in its Christian meaning. Balder represents that universal goodness, loyalty, affection, and harmony, which binds all beings to each other; Bragi, the poet, is his brother; Forseti, the peacemaker, is his son. But we shall but too soon have to return to him on a most melancholy occasion.

In spite of our desire to close this already too numerous list, we cannot well pass over in silence that poor Tyr, the very type of intrepidity and loyalty, who fell a victim to his own prowess and to his imprudent confidence in the other gods.

The latter, having one day met the wolf Fenris, invited him to enjoy a good meal with them. The wolf, always voraciously hungry, listened to the proposal. Then the Ases, pretending to fear that he might play them an ugly trick on the way home, insisted upon leading him by a chain around his neck, pledging their word as gods, however, that they would set him free upon going to table.

Fenris, suspicious as all wolves, in fact, as all wicked creatures are, consented to be bound, but made it a condition that as a proof of the good faith of the Ases, one of them should put his hand into his mouth. Tyr agreed to do so without hesitation, not expecting that personages of such lofty position could possibly be faithless. The gods,

however, did behave faithlessly and kept Fenris a
prisoner, whereupon the wolf claimed the fulfillment
of the pledge, and when Tyr put his hand into his
mouth, coolly bit it off up to the wrist. Hence
that particular joint has ever since been called *the
wolf's joint*, in memory of this inartistic amputa-
tion.

Thus the gods had a one-handed brother among
them, after having long been presided over by a
one-eyed god. But Tyr and Odin were by no
means the only gods who labored under such an
infirmity. Heimdall with the golden teeth must
evidently have had a set of false teeth ; Widar, the
god of silence, was dumb, and Hoder, that mysterious being whose name must not be pronounced by
any one, was blind. There was also a certain god,
called Herblinde, who was not only blind but —
actually dead! We poor mortals generally imagine
that death includes blindness as a matter of course,
but it was not so, apparently, among these mystic
personages. Herblinde, for instance, was quite blind,
although he was quite dead also, and yet he at-
tended the meetings of the gods and even had a
vote in their counsels. Do you understand that ?
I do not, I am sure.

And this grand council, this hospital of the Walhalla, which counted among its members a one-
handed and a dumb god, a toothless and two blind

gods, was, as I said, presided over by one-eyed
Odin! This fact recalls forcibly the old proverb:
Among the blind the one-eyed is king.

But why had. Odin but one eye?

Fortunately I am able, for once, to give an answer to this question.

Astronomers have naturally found a reply to this
Why? in their imperturbable system of sidereal
interpretations. Odin was the sun-god; the sun
was the eye of Nature, Nature had but one eye —
consequently Odin was bound to be born one-eyed!
. . . . Now you see why your daughter is deaf-
mute.

The Edda, however, gives a different account of
the matter, and I feel bound to adopt this explanation, as it is founded upon a knowledge of the
most secret mysteries.

Odin had two eyes when he was born, and the
sun was nothing more than his travelling companion, when he came from the far East, to revive
and warm the earth which had so long been in
the hands of the giants of the frost.

Several centuries after he had created man, he
was one day walking up and down in the lower
parts of his great ash tree Ygdrasil, and thinking
of the greatly increased responsibility which rested
upon him since he had added the government of
the earth to that of heaven, and since the earth

had begun to be peopled with a multitude of races. He was asking himself whether the knowledge of all things had been revealed to him fully enough to enable him satisfactorily to fill his two great offices. He had quaffed ample draughts by turns from the three vessels of Kvasir, but Eloquence, Poetry, and even Logic do not supply Wisdom.

As he passed by a large tank fed by a purling brook, he saw three beautiful swans swimming

merrily about in it, who after having examined him with half thoughtful, half mocking attention, twisted their long flexible necks in strange contortions and then seemed to converse with each other by significative glances.

He spoke to them and asked them if they possessed the secret of Wisdom.

The swans suddenly plunged beneath the surface,

and in their place there appeared three beautiful women, representing three different stages of life.

They were the Norns.

The first, called Urda, knew the Past; the second, called Verandi, saw the Present unfold itself before her eyes, hour by hour and minute by minute, and when to-day had become yesterday, her older sister gathered up the departed day and en-

tered it on her record. Finally Skulda, the third, the Norn of the Future, enjoyed the privilege of beholding with her far-seeing eyes the germs of all future events and of being able to foretell with unerring accuracy the date and the consequences of their occurrence.

Let us pause here a moment to notice a remark communicated to me by the amiable and learned

Dr. Rosalh, which may not be without interest to some of my readers.

It will be remembered that the Romans had at first pretended to recognize in these three Norns their own three Fates, probably because they were three and because they were women; at least I can see no other reason. Urda, Verandi, and Skulda were as beautiful and as graceful as the three Parcæ — Alecto, Lachesis, and Atropos — were ugly. Besides, their duties were entirely different. The Norns knew the fate of men, but they were utterly unable to lengthen human life. Such at least is the opinion of the great Holinshed in his Chronicles. Warburton sees in them nothing more than Valkyrias, but, what is far more astonishing, Shakespeare chose these three beautiful prophetic virgins, to furnish the three hideous, unclean, and toothless witches, the weird sisters, who called out to Macbeth, "All hail, Macbeth, that shalt be king hereafter!"

Shakespeare had evidently taken the curse denounced by the Church against the ancient deities in its literal meaning.

Odin had a better opinion of the three sisters; he conversed for some time with them, and afterwards came frequently back to visit them. It was thus and by their aid that he gained experience.

But even Experience, added to the precious gifts

11

of Eloquence, Poetry, and Logic, is not able to supply Wisdom.

He took counsel with the Norns, and in his

anxiety to possess this most precious of all gifts, he expressed his willingness to exchange for it, if needs be, his treasures of poetry and of eloquence, his magic armor which made him safe against all danger, his horse Sleipner, which had eight legs and crossed the air with the rapidity of lightning, his eagle and his vulture, his squirrel and his two

ravens. Then he went to Mimer, the wisest man
in existence, the successor of old Kvasir, and at-
tended his lectures like the most humble and zeal-
ous of students. When he had mastered the subject,
and felt that he had acquired Wisdom at last, he
paid the philosopher liberally by giving him one of
his own eyes, in order thus to show him the high
value he set upon the service which had been rendered to him by Mimer.

This was the reason why Odin was one-eyed.
The truth is far too honorable to the god to be
hid under idle astronomical pretexts.

Now, what use did he make of his wisdom?

He began by regulating the government of heaven.
The Ases had until now lived very much as they
chose; he now gave to each of them a duty to
perform : to Niord the management of rivers and
of fishing; to Egir, the seas and navigation; and
so to others, requiring regularity and accuracy of
all, but sternly prohibiting the display of extreme
zeal, just as Talleyrand used to do with his diplo-
matic apprentices.

Then he turned to the earth.

Here men had multiplied incessantly, and with
their numbers their wants had increased, and alas !
with these, their vices also ! In order to satisfy
the wants and to repress the vices, they had established among them that great, primitive law which

constitutes the whole code of laws among barbarians — the right of the stronger.

"TO EGIR, THE SEAS AND NAVIGATION."

The most fertile pastures, the rocks and grottoes
best fitted for dwellings and safe retreats, the forests that were richest in game and the springs
that were most frequented by the flocks, all were
taken by force and possession maintained by the
strength of the sword.

Wise Odin felt that violence gave no right and
that theft could not give a title to possession. He

determined to establish the right of property, and to give it, for greater efficiency, a religious character which would make it sacred in the eyes of nations.

One of his daughters, Gefione, was sent by him to one of the most powerful chiefs of Scandinavia. She presented herself before his tent, with presents in her hands. In return she asked only for a span of land. The chief gave her a vast but uncultivated territory.

Next she went, with secret purposes in her mind and always inspired by Odin, to a distant country, into the mountains, where giants dwelt. Here she married one of these giants, the most powerful of them all, to whom she bore four sons. The strong are apt to be gentle. Gefione took her four sons, changed them into oxen, and by words of gentle persuasion induced her husband to harness them

himself to a plough. A river marked the bound-ary of the field, on the other side stood an altar.

Thus was the first piece of property inaugurated,

by purchase, by labor, and under the protection of the gods. The first owner, the gigantic husband, represented Force submitting to Right, and the four oxen represented the hard-working family, improving the soil and enriching it with the sweat of their brow.

Soon people began to imitate Gefione's example, and in all directions land was measured and laid out; stones were put up to mark the boundary lines of each legal possession, and these stones were held sacred.

In order to encourage men in these efforts, the Ases made it a point every morning to show their bright, shining heads above the horizon and thus to cheer them by their presence and the interest they took in their labors.

The god Thor even came once to pay a visit to his sister Gefione, and then cast a few flashes of lightning upon each one of the newly acquired pieces of land, to render them sacred. Hence the old, deeply rooted notion that lightning hallows all it touches. Afterwards, and as late as the fifteenth century, it was deemed sufficient at Bonn, at Cologne, and at Mayence, to cast Thor's hammer upon the piece of land that had become a fief, in order to establish an absolute right of proprietorship.

But the right of property alone did not suffice to render human society stable and flourishing, —

the nations of the earth longed for a hierarchy of rank and race; at least the divine pupil of the wise Mimer decided it should be so. The means he employed to found such a hierarchy and the system itself appear curious and odd enough to us, who are no gods, but, unsuitable as they look now, they were successful at the time.

By his order Heimdall, the god with the false teeth, abandoned his post as guardian of the Walhalla for nine days, and after a long journey across the country, knocked at the door of a wretched tumbledown hut, where the *Great-grandmother* lived. Here he remained three days and three nights.

The Great-grandmother brought a male child into the world, black-skinned, broad-shouldered, with hard horny hands, and powerful arms. They called it *Thrall*, the serf.

Thrall's natural inclination led him to prefer the hard work in mines and in the wilderness; he was fond of the society of domestic animals and even slept with them in their stables. His sons became cattle-raisers, miners, or charcoal-burners.

Heimdall had continued his journey. He next stopped at the *Grandmother's* house, a small, simple cottage, but lacking in nothing that was useful. Here he remained three days and three nights.

The Grandmother gave birth to a son, who was called *Karl*, the free man.

Karl was fond of driving oxen under the yoke, of working in wood and in iron, of building boats and houses, and of trading. From him are descended our workmen and artisans, our merchants and builders.

Turning his face towards the south, Heimdall next went to a beautiful mansion, surrounded by magnificent gardens and reflected in the blue waters of a large lake. As the god had only to show his golden teeth in order to be welcomed by every woman he saw, the mistress of this mansion, the *Mother*, also received him with great delight and tried to do him honor. Dressed in her most costly robes she put an embroidered cloth upon a table of polished wood and offered him in silver dishes all the varieties of fish and game, in which the lake and the park near the house abounded. The Mother did everything to keep the god as long as possible at her house, but, as at the Grandmother's and at the Great-grandmother's, so he remained here only three days and three nights.

A son appeared to console the Mother for the departure of her illustrious guest; this child had at its birth already rosy cheeks, long hair, and a haughty look. When he was still a child, he was fond of brandishing his spear and of bending his bow; at fifteen he swam across the blue waters of the lake, or plunged on an unbroken horse into the depths of the forest, riding as fast as the wind. They called him Jarl, the noble.

Some years later Heimdall paid another visit to this country; delighted with the prowess of Jarl, he acknowledged him as his son and taught him the language of birds, which the gods alone understand and fluently speak. He taught him also the science of Runes, of runes of victory which are engraven on the blades of swords; runes of love to be traced upon drinking horns or the thumbnail; runes of the sea, with which the prow and the rudder of ships are decorated — in all cases precautionary measures by which alone ill fortune can be kept at bay.

Besides these gifts of knowledge, he bestowed upon him an inalienable, hereditary domain. This was the first entailed estate ever known in Europe.

Jarl, says the Edda, was a man of *eight-horse power.* Could we express it better in the noble railway Anglo-Saxon of our day, or does our modern English really go back to the old Scandinavian, as this coincidence would seem to prove?

Jarl's descendants are the great chieftains, the barons, princes, kings, and Druids, who have all inherited great power from their divine ancestor with the golden teeth. They alone are his legitimate and acknowledged children; the descendants of the grandmother and great-grandmother are illegitimate.

Still, whether acknowledged by the law or not, they all form a close chain, a single family, they all spring from the same god! Thus the humblest among them saw his rights secured for the future.

I must confess that, the more carefully I examine these barbarians, whether they were gods or men, the more I am surprised to discover beneath the outward cloak of their fables so many correct ideas of order and of justice. These fables had, of course, their day and then passed away. Up to the present time, it is true, there is not much of the day gone; perhaps also Odin may be blamed for having invented, before the world was a few hundred years old, both the Middle Ages and the Feudal System. But it would be wrong to blame him, for it must be acknowledged, that in spite of the violence of their manners and the bloody nature of their worship, a certain civilization had at last appeared among the Scandinavians. It may be called brutal, I grant; it may be called aggressive even, but it was after all an improvement, and it has held its own in the North, under snow and ice, like the vigorous plants of our Alps. How comes it that the Germans and the Franks, more favored by climate and by contact with highly civilized nations, remained so long inferior to the Scandinavians in this respect? Perhaps they were more liable to be invaded than the Sons of the North; the Scandinavians invaded the continent in all directions, but no one ever dreamt of invading their country.

After having thus established the right of property and a certain social hierarchy, Odin had next instituted marriage with the symbolic ring, and finally courts of justice.

But, since he had given to man an immortal soul, and since he held out to him reward or punishment in another world according to his deserts, Odin had been compelled to establish the first high tribunals in that other world.

We must, therefore, find our way to Walhalla and even to Hell, if the reader is disposed to follow us to that place.

VII.

VII.

WHEN the warriors were preparing for battle, a number of blue-eyed young maidens, mounted on bright, shining horses, passed through their ranks, animating them with word and gesture, and whispering into their ears warlike songs to be soon changed into triumphal chants for those who fell on the battlefield, mortally wounded.

These maidens were the Valkyrias, those Valky-

rias whom ever since the poets and painters of the Ossianic school have reproduced in a thousand forms. Nor must it be forgotten that this remarkable school, which the Scotchman Macpherson revived towards the end of the eighteenth century, counted among its most ardent admirers two enthusiastic Frenchmen, whose names were Napoleon and Lamartine.

These Valkyrias, beautiful nymphs of carnage as they were, delighted in the clash of arms, the shedding of blood, and the dying groans of the wounded, even in the odors exhaled by the dying, — a taste which seems little suited to fair, blue-eyed maidens. These unnatural tastes were, however, justified to a certain extent, by the peculiar mission which they had to fulfill, a mission of kindness and tender compassion. They walked to and fro on the battlefield, not to carry off the dead, but to gather the souls of those who had fallen. Of the *Scola* (such was the sweet name of the Soul among the nations of Germanic or Scandinavian race), they rapidly asked these questions : —

"Seola, did you belong to a free man or to a slave?

"Seola, did your master honor the gods and the priests of those gods?

"Did he keep his pledged word?

"Did he die like a brave man, with his face to the enemy and not a fear in his heart?

"Seola, did he ever fight against the men of his own blood and his own race?"

The human soul, as soon as it escapes from the

12

wretched bondage of this earth, no longer possesses the sad power of being able to tell a falsehood; Seola, therefore, answered these questions truthfully, even though it were to its own condemnation. In the latter case the Valkyrias left it to the black Alfs, a kind of demons who belonged to hell; but if the Seola had belonged to a brave and loyal warrior, the Valkyria instantly unfolded her white wings and took it to Walhalla, the home of the gods and the paradise of heroes.

This paradise, exclusively intended for free men, was still open to slaves also, if they had fallen by the side of their masters, or if they had thrown themselves voluntarily into the fire of the funeral pile for the purpose of continuing their service in the future life.

Let us see whether the delights of Walhalla were sufficiently attractive to warrant such self-immolation.

The one great enjoyment of all who dwell in Walhalla was combat and strife. That is a matter of taste, but did they not carry combat and strife a little too far? They fought there for hours and hours, with eagerness, with fury, even piercing each other and cutting each other to pieces to their hearts' delight. It is true, that as soon as the dinner hour came the blood ceased to flow, the wounds closed their gaping lips, the limbs that had been lopped off by the swords returned to their place, the broken heads and exposed entrails were restored without the surgeon's aid, not leaving a scar behind, and the heroes went arm in arm to dinner, looking forward with joy to a repetition of the same merry sport as soon as the meal should be finished.

The fare at this table of gods and heroes does not seem to have been peculiarly wholesome; at all events it was not very varied.

The pork-butchers' business was at that time uncommonly flourishing both in heaven and on earth. Tacitus tells us that among the races of the North, as far as the borders of the Baltic Sea, chieftains and matrons alike loved to wear suspended around their neck a small image of a pig as an emblem of abundance and fecundity. Rich and poor, all looked upon pork as the main supply of their pantry. The pig, however, was not deemed worthy to appear on Odin's table, and its place was taken by the boar: the gods lived upon wild boar, men upon domestic pig, that was the whole difference.

I am often tempted to eat pork, and I am occasionally enabled to taste wild boar; but I must solemnly confess, swearing if needs be by my stomach, that in my opinion, the gods and the heroes had by no means the best of it. It may

be, however, that wild boars here below are not
quite equal to heavenly boars.

However that may be, there appeared every

morning upon the edge of one of the marvelous
forests to be found in Walhalla, an enormous
colossal boar, a very mammoth of a boar. The

heroes proceeded to hunt it, accompanied at times by Thor, by Vali, the skillful archer, or by Tyr, the one-handed god, who nevertheless wielded his sword with power and accuracy. Then the monster was killed, cut up and roasted, and all dined together.

The next day there appeared on the edge of the marvelous forest another wild boar, quite as fat and quite as enormous, in fact in every respect as attractive as the boar of the day before — some think it was always the same animal, come to life

again. Then a new hunt and a new dinner upon roasted wild boar. Surely we poor people might become disgusted for the rest of our lives, one would imagine, — and those were immortal gods! What taste!

But there is worse behind yet. The Scandi-

navian paradise was by no means the only one
where the pork-butcher was thus glorified. In a
neighboring paradise, which the Finns had established, we are told by a learned writer, the rivers
were flowing with beer and hydromel, the *mountains consisted of lard and the hills of half-salted
pork.*

To help them in digesting their solid food, the
Scandinavian gods drank, like those of Finland,
great quantities of beer and hydromel; but they
had in addition, an abundance of wine which they
quaffed from gold cups. Wine! In this one word
thoughtful historians have discovered a whole revelation.

Now would it ever have occurred to Odin, in
his hyperborean lands, where the vine did not
exist and could not possibly live, to bring the fruit
of the vine to his paradise? Did he know grapes?
And when had he learnt to know them? But as I
do not wish to interrupt my story, I reserve the discussion of this great and important question, with
several others of the same kind, for another chapter, in which I hope to be able to develop my
views fully and scientifically.

Besides wine, beer, and hydromel, the blessed
people in Walhalla had an additional precious
beverage of their own, which it may safely be presumed, no mortal on earth has ever tasted. This

ambrosia of a novel nature was obtained by the
gods and heroes themselves, on certain favorable
days, from the white substance of the moon. Yes,
from the moon! Did they quaff it in full draughts
or did they inhale it through calumets? We do
not know, but the nations of the earth saw in these
periodical bleedings of the moon the reason for
her divers phases and her gradual diminution.
When she became reduced to a mere crescent,
fright was seen on all faces and oppressed all
hearts. Were the great people up there forgetting
themselves in their celestial orgies, and would they
drink up the moon to the last drop?

It must be borne in mind that they, like the
Germans, saw in the moon nothing but a transparent leathern bottle, filled with sweetened milk,
and phosphorescent.

Let us return now. To hunt the boar, to breakfast on wild boar, to dine on the same dish, day
after day, to drink beer and wine, and from time to
time that mulled egg which the moon furnished, to
fight morning and evening, to die and come to life
again, merely for the purpose of fighting again —
these were the amusements of that delightful
place. Upon my word, it took Scandinavians to
be content with such pleasures.

If Odin's paradise appears to us but little attractive, his hell, on the other hand, seems to have been

far from terrible, especially if we compare it with
the hell of some of our great poets, such as Dante
and Milton.

The hell of the Scandinavians occupied the
lowest depths of the world and consisted of two
parts, *Nastrond* and *Niflheim.* The latter is a
kind of dismal vestibule shrouded in darkness, in
which are seen wandering about the mournful
seolas of those who have been neither good nor
bad, neither heroes nor scoundrels, and of all who
have not fallen by the sword. To die on one's bed
or in an armchair, was a wrong in Odin's eyes, a
grievous wrong, though not exactly a crime, since
he punished it only with a temporary detention in
those damp, low places, where darkness, silence,
and weariness seemed to combine for their punishment. The dwellers in Niflheim had scarcely any
amusement except their reciprocal yawns, and from
time to time a flash of dim light which reached
there when the little black Alfs came in or went
out, busily engaged in conveying a load of souls.

The great criminals were thrown into Nastrond,
the real hell. What is very remarkable is, that
here there were no braziers and burning gridirons
to be seen, no furnaces and masses of flames as in
all the other hells. This was a hell of ice; it froze
here hard enough to split iron, and the damned
shivered with cold. Dante mentions something of

the kind in his great work, but between the Flor-
entine and the Scandinavian there can be no doubt
who borrowed from the other.

It was quite natural after all that in these win-
tery regions of Scandinavia, where cold is the greatest evil to be dreaded, intense, continued, eternal
cold should have become the terror and the punishment of the criminal. The idea of a hell of fire,

so far from keeping them from the fatal slope,
might very well have tempted some chilly scoun-
drel to commit a great crime.

The poor wretches who were shivering in Nas-

trond with stiffened hands and eyes full of frozen
tears, felt their tortures increased whenever Hela, the
pale goddess, the queen of that place, Death itself,
cast upon them a glance from her lack-lustre eyes.

Yes, it was Hela who reigned over this fright-
ful iceberg; her palace is called Misery, her gate
the Precipice, her reception room Grief, her bed
Disease, her table Famine, and her throne Male-
diction!

The body of this terrible queen is party-colored,
half white and half blue, and her breath is perfumed
with that horrible cadaverous odor in which the
Valkyrias delight.

But after all, the names seem to be worse than
the sufferings themselves ; for excessive cold par-
alyzes pain itself, and there is nothing here to
compare with those classic places where lava-baths,
rolling rocks, flaming wheels, horses of red-hot
iron, boiling pitch, fiery arrows and the snake whips
of the Eumenides made up an infernal stock of
tortures which might well tempt the imagination
of the greatest of poets.

In Nastrond there were no demons and no
Eumenides ; to be sure, there was a Bigvor and a
Sisvor, furies if you will have it so, watching at
the gates of hell, with the help of Gaun, the formidable dog, but all three are forbidden to enter
within.

The place of missing monsters is occupied by some of those whom Odin spared on the occasion of his first campaign against the giant sons of Ymer, and by the wolf Fenris, whom the Ases had treacherously captured. There are also two other wolves, convicted of having made an attempt upon the life of the Sun, and all of these monsters are firmly chained and appear rather as sufferers than as tormentors.

One of these days, their iron chains will be loosened; one of these days heaven will turn cold and hell will melt, and — then, woe to the gods!

Listen! The moment is drawing near when all these mysteries are to be solved. The hour is coming when *you shall hear*, when *you shall understand!* But before uttering these last words, final and at the same time fatal words, we must mention an event which at that moment occurred in the open assembly of the gods, filling heaven and earth with amazement, with pity and horror.

It must be acknowledged that so far the heavenly personages have appeared to be rather kindhearted and mild. Odin, in spite of his Druids and their demands for bloody sacrifices, seems to have been full of good intentions. The god Thor, with all his somewhat brutal ways, rendered great services to mankind; and the same hammer, which protected them against the giants, afterwards served,

without the aid of geometry, to mark the boundary
lines of their respective properties. The golden-
teethed god, Heimdall, gave most undoubted evidence of his devotion to the human race and of
his self-denial in his visits to the Grandmother and
the Great-grandmother, and so did the other gods.
But we had good reasons for not going through
the whole list of the Ases. For there is one
whom we keep in reserve so that he may appear
at the right hour, and that is Loki, the god of evil
and the genius of destruction.

Surpassing Odin himself in his magic skill, fair
of form and features, a smile on his lips — thin
lips, however, the Edda adds — and apparently possessed of the most jovial temper so as to make him
a most agreeable person, Loki is in reality a com-
pound of the most hideous vices. He is the rep-
resentative of hatred and cruelty, of envy, hypoc-
risy, and perversity. In fact, he is our Satan, before
the fall. If he had been king of hell, Miflheim and
Nastrond would both have been filled with more
tortures and more horrors than all the other hells
which are known to men.

And yet he was the god upon whom the dwellers
in Walhalla counted for their entertainment, and
whom they had surnamed the Clown!

One day an ancient prophetess returns to life,
rises in her grave, and utters a terrible cry: " Balder,

fair Balder, is going to die!" With these words she falls back again upon her mournful couch and dies again — forever.

In the meantime this cry has been heard even at the top of the ash Ygdrasil. The Ases are troubled and amazed; they meet, they look at each other, thoroughly frightened, for on the life of Balder depends the existence of all the other gods. Moreover, Balder the Bright is the glory of heaven and the love of the earth. Can Balder die, the most charming and the purest as well as the most beautiful of all the sons of Odin? He, who was so beautiful that Hela herself could not help smiling when she looked at him — he, so pure that no falsehood could be uttered in his presence and that a vessel containing an adulterated liquid would break instantly at his approach — he, so charming that all the gods love him as their favorite child, and that men have surnamed him Hope? No, no! Balder shall not die, said the Ases.

His distressed mother Frigg, Odin's wife, shows her apprehensions by her intense anguish, and her sobs scarcely allow her to speak. She tells those who try to laugh at the sudden alarm of all who have heard the warning of the prophetess, that for several nights already she has been repeatedly, persistently warned in her dreams of the death of her well-beloved son. She would not believe it, she adds, but now she does believe.

The divine sybil Vola, whose predictions have never proved untrue, and Skulda, the Norn of the Future, are summoned to appear. They consult with each other and this is their decision : —

" Balder is in danger; Balder will die unless all earthly substances that can inflict death, are rendered powerless."

Frigg descends to the earth and speaks to volcanoes and water-spouts, to frost and hail, and they
promise to spare her son. Among the aquatic
powers, from the ocean to the smallest brook,
among the stones, from the mightiest rock to the
pebble, and among the metals, from gold to iron,
there is none that does not swear the same oath.
The plants also promise, from the oak to the smallest shrub and down to the humblest grass.

Triumphantly she returns to heaven to announce
the good news. Everybody is overjoyed. They
celebrate the happy result of her journey by a
family dinner, at which Loki succeeds in exhilarat-
ing even Odin himself by
his merry jokes. He had
never appeared in better
spirits ; had never seemed
to sympathize more warmly
with the happy court.

When the feast was
ended and the last cups
were drained in honor of
Balder, some one proposed
for the general amusement
to try how far all these substances, vegetable or min-
eral, will be faithful to the oath they have sworn,
when brought face to face with Balder.

Beginning with the most inoffensive of them all, they throw at him a clod of earth; the clod of earth breaks into a cloud of dust before it touches him. Then they pour a pitcher of water over him and the water forms a cascade above him without wetting even his garments. They try to strike

him with a hazel wand; the wand, slipping from the hand that holds it, breaks in two. Balder is amused by the game and encourages the bystanders to renew their attacks.

The skillful Uller shoots at him a pointless arrow, aiming, from excessive caution, only at his shoulder. The arrow passes at a distance of twenty feet from its aim and continues its flight through

the air, like a bird in search of its prey beyond
the clouds.

Ten other assailants meet the same fate, trying
their luck with a fragment of rock and a heavy
branch in the shape of a club. But the fragment
was of stone and remembered the promise given to
Frigg, and the club was cut from a tree and the
tree remembered the promise given to Frigg.

Encouraged by so many reassuring trials, Freyr
desired to try his magic sword, but for once the
faithful sword was deaf to his orders. Thor bran-
dished his hammer, but the hammer suddenly
reversed its action and well nigh made him fall
back upon his heels. Freyr's sword and Thor's
hammer were both of iron and the iron remembered the promise given to Frigg.

Loki took care not to appear.

The sport was over, as it seemed, when suddenly
the blind god Hoder, Balder's own brother, was
seen to advance, feeling his way, towards the bright
god. Hoder held in his hand a small bunch of
leaves, a bit of grass, at least it appeared such
after the fearful instruments that had just been
brought into play.

Immense laughter, a laughter such as the gods
of Homer were in the habit of enjoying, broke
out at the sight; Loki laughed till his sides shook
and Hoder himself shared the general hilarity.

13

But he drew nearer and nearer, shaking his bit of verdure in the air; then, almost tottering and having learnt from the bystanders in what direction he would have to turn, he threw the slender twig against Balder, using his full force, which was prodigious.

He hit Balder full in the chest and the god fell instantly. That bright light which was always shining around him became extinct; he closed his eyes, and lowered his beautiful brow deprived of its glory. . . . . Balder was dead!

He had been struck by a bit of mistletoe. Frigg had addressed her prayers to the oak tree, but she had not thought of the mistletoe which grows on the oak tree ; the mistletoe had given no promise to Frigg. Must we look here for a symbolic meaning? Did this mean, that the Druidical mistletoe was soon to triumph over the gods of Scandinavia? This could not be so, for at the time to which we have come, there was no trace left of the wise worship of the Druids of the first epoch; the Druids of the second epoch were fast losing their power, and the Scandinavian gods were daily increasing in popularity, even beyond the banks of the Rhine.

But we ought not to interrupt this account of Balder's death, which is as poetical and as touching as the most famous fables of Greece.

When blind Hoder, whose name must not be uttered, you remember, hears the cries of despair which break out all around him, and encircle him on all sides with maledictions, he is troubled and seriously distressed. Then, all of a sudden joining in the distressed cries of the Ases, he falls utterly overcome upon his brother's body and denounces Loki as the author of this calamity. Loki has reproached him for being the only one who took no part in the amusements by which they thought to honor Balder, and he it was who had not only given him the fatal plant but who had also directed his arm. Loki was jealous of all the perfections of Balder and he hated him as much as the other gods loved him.

They look for Loki, but he has disappeared. No doubt he has tried to escape from the vengeance of the Ases by seeking refuge in the mountains among the giants, his natural allies, or perhaps in the deep sea, with the serpent Iormungandur. And whilst they thus lament, inquire, and investigate, Balder's soul is carried off by the black Alfs to Niflheim, the dark vestibule of hell.

Odin still cherished hopes that his dead son might be restored to him. Upon his order Hermode, the messenger of the gods, mounts his horse Sleipner and goes to see Hela, but neither promises nor threats can move the dread goddess. Fate has decided, and Fate is above the gods, as the gods are above men.

Then Frigg herself goes to see the pale goddess. Frigg weeps and the merciless goddess is unable to keep her heart from softening when she sees the tears of such a mother. She says to her : —

"Let all created beings — mind, I say, all created beings ! — give a tear to Balder, a tear such as you have shed in my presence, and Balder shall be restored to you !"

Frigg was unwilling to trust any one but herself with the effort to realize such hopes. Once more she went over the world, gathering around her all the races of men, one after the other, and as she mentioned the name of Balder, tears flowed from all eyes.

For three months she visited all the forests and all the mountains, the seas and the lakes and the animals that live in the waters and the mountains; and seas and lakes and mountains wept. She went even to the abode of the giants, the enemies of the gods, and her grief made the giants also weep; every tree wept and every rock wept.

Frigg thought her task was accomplished, and was filled with joy; but she heard that in the far East of Midgard there lived an old woman in the heart of a forest of iron trees. As she lived alone there, far from any beaten track, she had never become known to the intrepid traveller. Now, however, Frigg sought her out by steep paths, cut up with gullies and fierce torrents, and at last

found her. When the mother told her pitiful tale, the iron trees wept, but the old woman would not weep.

They called her Thorck, and her heart was ten times as hard as her name.

" What do I care for your Balder ? " she cried ; " what do I care whether he is dead or alive ? You have other sons ; I have not one left me. Once I had four, and all four were my pride, my delight. They were so fair ! They were so tall ! Your son Thor killed every one of them. I wept much at that time. Now, it is all over. Look for tears elsewhere, I have no tears to give to other people's sorrows ! "

Frigg bowed down before her, begged her, conjured her, and even fell on her knees before her ; but the old woman was inflexible. Balder had to remain a prisoner with Hela.

Some interpreters of Scandinavian runes have been of the opinion that the bereaved mother in the forest of iron trees was none other than Loki himself, changed into an old woman. That thought, however, is inadmissible. The Ases were beyond the reach of Hela, and Loki's refusal would not have rendered void the unanimous vote of all Nature, when tears of pity and sympathy alone were to be given as votes. It is much more plausible to suppose, that Loki had induced Thorck to refuse by his counsels and by his enchantments ; through him the heart of the old woman had become iron as well as the trees of the forest in which she lived. Thus Loki had twice caused the death of Balder!

It was at this time that a strange, almost incredible report was for the first time heard among men. The Druids whispered it cautiously into the ears of the initiated, and voices were said to utter it in the air during the night. This report, a terrible secret, a most unexpected revelation, stated that the gods were about to die! Thor would die, after seeing lightning become extinct in his hands; Odin himself would die, and so would the others. The fate of each one of them was depending on the fate of this fragile world over which they ruled, and this world had to perish because Balder had perished.

What? Should the Universe change back into chaos? Was there no all-powerful will that could arrest the process of destruction before it was too late? But where could such omnipotent will be found, now that the gods were no longer to be in existence?

Listen! listen to these verses from the Edda!

"Who is the most ancient among the gods?

"Alfader, that is, the universal father. He has always been and will ever be; he governs all things, both big and small; he has made the heavens, the earth and the gods. Odin created man, but Alfader gave him his immortal soul!"

Thus we come back to the pure essence of an only god, who is ever the same, whether his name be Teut, Esus, or Jehovah ; the other gods are nothing but emanations proceeding from him, living symbols intended to 'live for a few thousand centuries — that is all.

Do you hear ? Do you understand now ?

Do ‚you understand why the great ash tree Ygdrasil is continually gnawed at its root by a dragon ? Why four famished stags feed upon its foliage ? You understand ? Well !

But by what sign shall we recognize the approaching end of the gods — that which the Edda calls their *twilight ?*

The most important among all the sacred books of the North, a volume containing the prophecies of the divine sybil Vola, the *Voluspa*, will tell you.

" When the fatal moment draws near, their voice will cease to be able to utter the accustomed chants, and the luminous brightness radiating from their bodies will fade away little by little.

" When they leave their bath, their bodies will not dry at once, as they do now, but remain moist ; drops of water will continually drip from them, and they will in this respect become like unto mortal men.

‚ " In order to overcome these first symptoms of

indisposition, the wife of the god Bragi, Iduna, will give them certain apples to eat, which she keeps in reserve. These apples will have the effect of strengthening them and of restoring to them a kind of fictitious youth for a few thousand years perhaps.

" One day, however, their eyes will begin to wink; the next morning, upon awaking, their eyelids will be found closed, and then they will turn red and blear.

" At table, when proceeding to their usual libations, their slightly tremulous hands will be unable to hold their cups steadily; some of the wine or the hydromel will escape and their garments will remain stained.

" Woe to them if a grain of dust adheres to these stained garments !

" Woe to them still more, if the wreaths of flowers or of jewels begin to fade and to wither on their brows !

" Finally, when the sweet perfumes which now are exhaled from their bodies, change into acrid and sickening odors, there will be nothing left for them but to make their last will."

I am well convinced that this last phrase has been stealthily introduced into the Voluspa by some kind of criminal and fraudulent trick. The rest, however, is a faithful translation of the original text, as taken from the best authenticated editions.

"Then," the prophecy continues, "then three sacred cocks, dwelling in the three principal worlds,

will crow and reply to each other, announcing the *Twilight of Greatness.*

"Then, everything on earth will be in disorder and confusion ; families will be at variance with each other, the claims of blood will no longer be acknowledged, and brothers will be arrayed against brothers.

"Adultery and incest, robbery and murder, will prevail among men, and the age will be an age of barbarism, an age of the sword, an age of tempests, an age of wolves!

"The wolves will be ready to devour the sun. Three long winters, with no summers between them, will cover the earth with snow and ice; the branches of the trees will give way under the immense burden; the sun will be darkened more and more; the moon will dissolve into vapor and the stars will go out; the mountains, shaking in their foundations, will ·be tossed to and fro like reeds in a river; the earth will reject all the plants, the trees, and the rocks which it now bears; the waters will cast the fish upon the shore and with them their algae, their corals, and even the bodies of shipwrecked men, hideous skeletons, whose rattling bones will chime in grimly with the warning of the rising flood.

"Then the sea will grow dark, and upon its waters there will be seen floating that monstrous ship made of the nails of dead men. At the rudder, Ymer, the giant, will stand, having been recalled to life for a time, in order to assist Loki in scaling the heavens by the way of Bifrost, the rainbow, at the head of the other Giants of the Frost.

"Then Surtur the Black will arrive from the southern regions, from the realm of fire, with all of his malignant demons, bearing torches and ready to set heaven and earth on fire.

"Then Hela, the pale goddess of death, will set free her prisoners, the wolf Fenris first of all, and march at the head of these monsters to assist the powers of the South.

"Then the gods will take up their arms; Odin will gather them around him, and with them the heroes from Walhalla; and the last battle will be fought."

But Vola's prophecy has to be fulfilled; the gods must perish, and the world with them.

Freyr dies in the flames of Surtur the Black; Thor succumbs to the deadly embrace and the poisonous bites of the great serpent Iormungandur; but, before dying, he kills it. Odin is torn to pieces by the wolf Fenris.

During the struggle, the heavens have been scaled and the genii of fire enter on horseback through the breach, while the giants shake the ash Ygdrasil, which writhes uttering long sighs, and at last falls with the heavenly vault which it has been upholding. The conquerors and the conquered alike are crushed under the ruins, and the world being set on fire by Surtur the Black, vanishes in smoke.

Thus the night of the gods has to succeed to the twilight of the gods.

" O you, spirits of the mountains, do you know whether anything will continue to exist?" asks the Voluspa, at the end of these mournful prophecies.

It must be admitted that this sombre and terrible conception is not without a certain poetic grandeur, a certain savage heroism, which we cannot help admiring. In these verses the Edda is in no way inferior to the most brilliant pictures drawn by Dante or by Milton, and more than once it approaches nearly to the Apocalypse. Thus, as the inspired Apostle saw a new heaven and a new earth, the Edda also announces the coming of a time, when a new earth, more favored and more perfect than ours, shall succeed the old earth.

" When the earth is thus broken to pieces and devoured by fire, what shall happen next?

" There will come forth from the sea another earth, more beautiful and more perfect.

" And will any of the gods survive?

" Balder will be revived and come forth from the place of departed spirits, to rule over the new world under the guidance of the imperishable Al-fader.

" Then will be the reign of Justice."

The mythology of the Scandinavians embraces, as we have shown, among its symbols all the great phenomena of Nature, the continual struggle between the two opposite principles, creation and destruction. Being, besides, more complicated and more intelligent than the mythology of the Gauls and the Germans, it deserved to fill a large space in our work, and such a space we have accorded it cheerfully.

But why was it that the civilization introduced by Odin contributed as little as the philosophy of the Druids to the real well-being and the improvement of mankind? I think I see the reason.

In the eyes of the German as well as of the Scandinavian, God was only just and rigid. The rule of the God of Love had not yet begun. Perhaps Balder was to inaugurate it in that other world which the Edda announced.

Do you hear? Do you understand?

Amid all the incidents which were to mark the general conflagration, there is one which particularly recalls to our mind a great historical event. Alexander of Macedonia once questioned certain Celtic ambassadors and was told by them, that what they feared most upon earth, was the falling down of the sky.

This apparently lofty answer filled the young

conqueror with admiration, and it is still admired by modern students of history. It was, however, in reality nothing more than a simple, naïve rendering of one of their articles of faith; for all their prophetic books threatened them with the destruction of the heavens.

Another detail, the complete destruction of this globe of ours, after a series of fearful catastrophes, recalls to me, not exactly a great historical fact, but a simple game of my childhood, which may have been symbolic, nay, which may have come down to us from the Edda. This, however, I state with great hesitation.

Did you ever know one of the merriest games, which was once very much the fashion in city and country alike, when a firebrand, a burning stick, or a bunch of straw set on fire, was quickly passed from hand to hand? To prevent its going out, while you held it, you were bound to pass it as quickly as possible to your neighbor, repeating at the same time the expressive words: "*The little fellow is still alive.*" Your neighbor passed it to his neighbor and thus it travelled all around, always accompanied by the same, constant burden: "The little fellow is still alive!" This game was transformed during the Middle Ages, in the North, and especially in Bretagne, into the Torch Dance, as I have mentioned before.

Now I imagine that this game, in some way or other, prefigured the universal conflagration that was to come, and *the little fellow* was the world.

But we must make haste to reach our great scientific discussion.

VIII.

14

VIII.

How the Gods of India live only for a Kalpa, that is, for the Time between one World and another. — How the God Vishnu was One-eyed. — How Celts and Scandinavians believed in Metempsychosis, like the Indians. — How Odin, with his Emanations, came forth from the God Buddha. — About Mahabarata and Ramayana. — Chronology. — The World's Age. — Comparative Tables. — Quotations. — Supporting Evidence. — A Cenotaph.

My reader has had a lucky escape.

Determined as I was to fathom in this chapter the true origin of the Scandinavian religion, and inspired by the zeal of a recent convert, I had collected and compared every document that could aid me in proving the Oriental descent of the priests of Odin as well as of the other Druids. I thought it was a beautiful doctrine, and especially an entirely new one.

When I finished my chapter, which I thought was exceedingly well done, I read it to Doctor Rosahl, expecting, I must confess, to be warmly congratulated.

"Why, my dear sir," he said, when I had finished, "you have made great efforts to prove a thing which has been established long since. All the master minds of France and Germany, to say nothing of other nations, agree on that subject. I mean men like Fauriel, Lassen, Lenormand, Ampère, Eichhoff, Saint-Marc Girardin, Marmier, Klaproth, Ozanam, the two Rémusats, the two Thierrys, the two Humboldts, the two Grimms, not to mention twenty others.

"Why will you come to their assistance after they have won the victory? Do you merely wish to display your scholarship?"

I indignantly denied the charge, and seizing my manuscript with both hands, I resolutely threw it into the fire.

A remnant of paternal weakness induced me, however, to retain the summary of that famous chapter, and I have inserted it here in its regular place, so that it might bear evidence of my wasted labor. As the *corpus delicti* is no longer in existence, this summary may stand there like an inscription on an empty tomb, to honor the memory of the deceased.

My VIIIth chapter is thus changed into a cenotaph.

I — a scholar! Great God! Let the reader not be disturbed. My purpose in writing this work was nothing more than to try and collect along the banks of the Rhine all the curious myths which have survived the ancient creeds of Europe; for they have all come to the great river. There the traveller finds piled up, after the manner of alluvial layers, all the ancient fables, all the marvelous and often childish tales to which the credulity and lively imagination of our forefathers gave a ready welcome. With the exception of a very few cases, in which the grave nature of the subject lifts me necessarily into higher regions, I wish mainly to tell you once more *Grandmamma's Tales.* That is what we are going to do next. The Edda itself has no other meaning, for *Edda* means the same as our *grandmother.*

No, I am too great a lover of tales of a tub ever to have claimed the reputation of being a scholar; but at times I like to glean a little where scholars have reaped. I have been shown the best spots, and I pilfer as well as I can — that is all.

An ignoramus and a pilferer, I resemble a bee which might fly into a botanical garden and, utterly

unacquainted with the Latin names of flowers, carry
off joyously a rich harvest, without pretending to be
able to make academic honey.

IX.

IX.

IT is high time for us to return to the banks of
the Rhine, where the two religions of Jupiter and
Odin were about to meet face to face.

At that time the terrible prophecies of the Edda were far from being near their fulfillment; Odin had a long period of omnipotence yet before him.

To the great surprise of the adversaries, the Romans, so far from showing any alarm at his approach, received him and his retinue of deities as old acquaintances.

According to their unchanging policy they would see in him nothing but a Jupiter, and in fierce Thor another gallant Mars, somewhat sobered by a long residence in northern countries and excessive use of beer.

The Romans looked, in fact, upon all of these Scandinavian gods and goddesses simply as upon myths of their own that came back to them once more.

The poets hallowed these claims and the historians tried to justify them. According to some, Odin the Conqueror, a member of the family of Ases, had first given to some of his conquests the name of Asia (which might very well be so), and then receded before the Roman armies to cold hyperborean regions. Here he had adopted the gods of his new conquerors, hoping that they would, in return, make him victorious — which seems to me in the highest degree improbable. According to others, the poet Ovid, when Augustus had banished him to Scythia, had learnt the language of the bar-

barians, among whom he was living, and finding
them willing and eager to listen to him, had recited
before them his "Metamorphoses." This was all

that was needed to induce the Scythians to make
for themselves gods after the model of the Roman
gods.

Tacitus, Plutarch, Strabo, and a host of the most
illustrious writers never hesitated to give currency
to such childish stories, ignoring entirely the date
of the Scandinavian religion.

As Rome, however, permitted no human sacrifices, the priests of Odin and of Teut had at first
withdrawn far from the beaten track, into the
depths of dark old forests. There they could live
quietly, practice without restraint the religion of
their forefathers, and kill their men in perfect secu-
rity. At least such were their hopes. The Roman
soldiers, however, who handled the woodman's axe

as readily as the sword, and the spade as well as
the spear, soon made big holes in these venerable

forests, murdered the murderers, and overthrew
their blood-stained altars.

Occasionally it happened that the brave legionaries who were employed in these hazardous enterprises, did not reappear. The proconsuls, whose duty it was to keep Germany in order, would have liked to inflict severe punishment; but just then the great reaction began to set in, from the North against the South.

Whilst Rome was making efforts to establish her power in Germany, certain German tribes, Franks and Burgundians, invaded France and began to settle down in some of the conquered Roman provinces. The proconsuls thought it both prudent and wise not to raise the question of religion; and for a long time a truce was tacitly agreed upon between all the different creeds, though not without some misgivings on both sides. Odin had his altars by the side of those of Jupiter; a temple in honor of Thor stood facing a temple dedicated to Mars, and if Bacchus, Diana, and Apollo had their sacred days, Bragi, Frigg, and Freya had theirs also.

In spite of this general toleration, the parties watched each other carefully.

Sooner or later a holy war had to break out; in certain regions it had already begun, when fishermen of the Rhine busily drawing in their nets, heard, for the first time, a still small voice coming down upon them on the waters of the river, which whispered the names of Jesus and Mary.

The same voice and the same names were simultaneously heard again and again before Strasbourg,

Mayence, and Cologne. It was Christianity that was approaching.

These wondrous words, which now the river only

murmured, had soon after been forced by some mystic power from the lips of the Druidesses in their prophetic exaltation and from the priests of Jupiter, as they consulted their auguries.

There was a Druid, who, in the act of sacrificing, was suddenly seized with inspiration, and dropping the bloody knife felt impelled to cry out: *Miserere mei, Jesus !* and yet Latin had until then been an unknown tongue among the Druids !

The nations stood expectant, waiting for the revelation of a new faith.

Soon a number of fugitives from Tolbiac, returning to the Rhine, produced consternation in all hearts by the announcement that Clovis, the king of the Franks, who had long been suspected of a secret understanding with Rome, had gone over to the god of the Christians, and that the god of the Christians was at that moment advancing at the head of ten legions of destroying angels.

When this news came, the rival religions laid aside their jealousy, and terrified by a common danger, joined hands to resist the invader. A general appeal was made not only by the followers of Odin to those of Jupiter, but also to the Northern gods, the Finnish gods, the Russian gods, and the Slavic gods. The danger was threatening to all alike, and they responded to the appeal and came to the Rhine.

We cannot so rapidly pass over this vast Olympian assembly of gods, a poet's dream, it may be,

but a traditional dream, full of strange and striking splendor, which completes in a most unexpected manner the limited description we have tried to give of Northern Myths.

At this grand meeting there appeared in the first place a goodly number of Borussian or Prussian gods, among whom stood first and foremost Percunos, the divine leader of the heavenly bodies; Pikollos, whose face was as pale as Hela's and whose duty was, like hers, to preside over hell; exacting, however, from men nothing but prayers accompanied by beating hearts, he cared nothing whether he was feared or beloved. A third god, Potrympos, had the appearance of a youth, with smiling lips and with a wreath of wheat ears and flowers on his brow; this was the god of War. Of War? And what meant the smile on his lips and, the wheat ears on his brow? They indicated that he was also the god of public supplies and even of love.

It seems that, in ancient Prussia, War was the purveyor-general and supplied everything.

In the retinue of this great trio, we find Antrympos, the god of seas and lakes; Poculos, the god of the air and of storms; then, after these gods ending in *os*, came other deities ending in *us ;* Pilvitus, the god of riches, Auchwitus, the god of the sick, and Marcopulus, the god of the nobles. The latter was the terror of the common people, whom he held under an iron yoke. In order to

15

conciliate his good will, they prayed to Puscatus, another god in *us*, but a kindhearted god. He lived under an elder tree, and the price he exacted in return for his mediation was the modest gift of a piece of bread and a *schoppen* of beer.

Although their priests were called Crives or Waidelottes, their ceremonies were, nevertheless, mere imitations of those of the Druids. The Borussians honored particularly the famous oak of Remowe, to which Percunos, Pikollos, and Potrympos paid a daily visit. To these same gods they offered their prisoners of war; but they were not sacrificed by means of a knife after the German o'r the Scandinavian manner. They destroyed them by fire or they gave them to be devoured to enormous serpents who lived upon the altar and for the altar.

Now all these gods have come to Germany accompanied by their monstrous reptiles, by griffins

fearful to behold, and by demons summoned from hell, all called upon to take part in the impending struggle.

Almost at the same time with the Prussian gods
arrived also the Scythian gods and those of the
Sarmatians, the former in chariots, according to
the manner of travelling which prevailed among
those nations. They also bowed low, like their people, before the all-powerful Tabiti, the great repre-
sentative of their religion, Fire. The Scythians
had evidently derived very little profit from hearing
Ovid read his " Metamorphoses."

The others were but few in numbers ; their
representatives were their chief triad : Perun, their
Jupiter Tonans ; Rujewit, who controlled the clouds ;
and Sujatowist, the judge of the dead. These three
brought in their train only Trizbog and the Tassanis, that is, the plague and the furies. Their
other gods, unable to do anything for success in
war, had wisely stayed at home.

Can I neglect mentioning the names and attributes of these inoffensive local deities, whom the
fierce Sarmatians worshipped. They were : —

Kirnis, who causes the cherries to ripen ;

Sardona, who watches over the nut trees ;

Austeïa, who presides over the education of bees ;

The sweet Kolna, who sees to the marriage of
flowers.

There were also gods or goddesses of corn, of
the kneading-tub and the wash-tub, the god of flies
and the god of butterflies ; we must confess that

these deities could hardly have been very useful on the banks of the Rhine.

But Odin and Jupiter could count upon more efficient and more reliable allies in the gods of Finland.

The gods bear almost always the impress of the character of their followers and of those over whom they rule, and what other nation has ever given such proofs of undaunted courage as the Finns or Finlanders? Pirates on the Baltic, as the Scandinavians were pirates on the ocean, they shared with them the booty that could be gotten in all the Northern seas. They had originally come from the high table-lands of Asia, together with their brethren the Turks, the Mongols, and the Tartars; their first appearance was made under the name of Ugorians or Ogres, and surely the Ogres have made a lasting and a terrible impression on our popular tales!

The Finns consisted almost exclusively of sailors and soldiers, of miners and blacksmiths. To smelt iron and to fashion it into anchors for their ships, into lances, swords, and spears, was their principal occupation. Hence they paid special reverence to Rauta-Rekhi, the personification of iron; to Wulangoinen, the father of iron, and to Ruojuota, the nurse of iron. They worshipped in like manner with special zeal three sombre virgins, whose powerful breasts were running over with a dark milk, which turned into iron as it cooled off, as water turns into ice when it cools off.

Their principal gods, besides these whom I have mentioned, were again three, and, as usual, three brothers.

The oldest, Vainamoinen, of hoary age, created celestial and terrestial fire, that is to say, the sun and the volcanoes.

The second, Ukko, has to provide them with fire, so as to prevent the earth from returning to the condition of an immense icicle, and the sun to the form of a heap of extinct embers. Living in the clouds he now blows upon the sun and now upon the volcanoes so as to keep up the blaze in both, and encourages them with his voice, the thunder.

Ilmarinnen, the third, a very industrious and most skillful workman, has forged the earth and the seven heavens by which it is surrounded; hence he is called the *Eternal Blacksmith.* He spends his life at the forge, making sometimes stars of all sizes and at other times spare moons. He has even made a silver woman, not for himself, however, but for a younger brother, whose manifold and incessant occupations left him no time to take the necessary steps for a suitable marriage. This woman of fine metal, well-made, beautiful, charming, and of the sweetest disposition, had but one single defect, — no

one could come near her without being chilled to
the marrow of his bones.

However, the most skillful blacksmith cannot be
expected to make a perfect woman at the first
trial.

When the question of his own marriage was
mooted, Ilmarinnen preferred taking a ready made
wife, and, according to the usage which prevailed
among the Finns as well as among the Germans, he
bought one.

For the sake of enjoying some relief after such
a long enumeration of deities, now entirely out of
fashion, I feel strongly tempted to insert here *a
saga*, a Finnish legend, which treats of this very
marriage of Ilmarinnen, the blacksmith, and was
composed by his own sister. In this wedding-song,
which is full of the sweetest and chastest sentiments, she exhibits the domestic life of these arti-
san-gods, who sometimes were disposed to beat
their wives, — at least the saga suggests the occurrence of such events.

Ilmarinnen has just been married and becomes
impatient, he actually swears at not seeing his
young bride come to him in great haste. Listen
to what is sung to him, with an accompaniment
on a small Kantele guitar, by his sister, the hostess
of Pohjola, in order to calm him the better: —

"O husband, brother of my brothers, you have

already waited long for the coming of this happy day; wait patiently a little longer. Your well be-loved will not tarry long. She finishes her toilet; but you know it is far to the fountain to which she has to go for water.

"O husband, brother of my brothers, be patient! She has just put on her robe, but she has only put on one sleeve. You would surely not have her appear before you with one sleeve empty?

"O husband, she has just arranged her hair; a beautiful belt encircles her waist, but she has a shoe only on one foot; she must needs have time to put on the other shoe also.

"Husband, ... here she is coming, ... but she has put on only one glove, ... give her time to put on the other!"

When the young bride appears at last, the good hostess of Pohjola is suddenly deeply concerned for her : —

"O wife, O purchased maid, O dove that has been sold! My sister, my poem, my green branch, how many tears you will shed!

"Your family were very eager to have the money paid down for you in the hollow of a shield.

"Poor ignorant girl, you thought you were leaving the paternal roof for a few hours, for a day, perhaps! Alas! You have surrendered forever, you have a master now!"

And then turning once more to Ilmarinnen, she adds : —

" O husband, brother of my brothers, do not teach this child, the slave, whip in hand, the way she must walk.

" Do not make her cry under the rod or under the stick; teach her gently, in a soft voice, with closed doors.

" The first year by words, the second year by a frown, the third year by gently pressing her foot. Be patient!

" If, after three years, she is unwilling to learn, O husband, brother of my brothers, take a few slender reeds, take a little broom-sedge, chastise her, but with a rod covered with wool.

" If she still resists, well ; cut a twig in the woods, a willow branch, not too stout, and hide it beneath your garment. Let no one guess what is going to happen.

" Above all, do not strike her hands nor her face; for her brother might well ask you: Has a wolf bitten her? Her father might well say to you: Has a bear torn her thus?"

Does not this Saga, with all its harsh allusions, breathe a most touching tenderness? It seems that the most delicate sentiments were preserved intact amid the coarsest manners and the most violent passions. What was your name, O naïve muse of

Finland, who inspired the good hostess of Pohjola?
Were you not perhaps a daughter of those beautiful Indian gandharvas, who said, —

"The elephant is led by a rope, the horse by a
bridle, and a woman by her heart."

And does it not remind us of our humble and
simple-minded neighbors, when we hear how this
Eternal Blacksmith, this first-class god who has
made heaven and earth, who buys a wife and beats
her, expresses his fear of the reproaches of his
brother-in-law and his father-in-law?

After this pause we must go on describing the
other armies of gods who had hastened to the
banks of the Rhine in order to resist a common
enemy.

By the side of the heavenly representatives of
Scythia and Sarmatia, of Prussia and Finland, we
find other gods belonging to the different Slavonic
races. But why should we repeat here a complete
list of all this multitude of allies, whose curious
names the most retentive memory could not possibly retain?

Suffice it to say that the Lithuanians, the Mo-
ravians, the Silesians, Bohemians, and Russians
were represented at this meeting by their most formidable deities. There was Ilia, the great archer,
whose arrows hit the mark after having passed
through a thickness of nine fir trees; Radgost, the

merciless destroyer; Flintz, the skeleton god, who
bore a lion's head on his shoulders and drove a
chariot of flames; and the giant Yaga-Baba, whose
head reached high above the loftiest mountains.
When a warrior was seized with fear before he be-
held the enemy, he immediately took him from the
ranks and brayed him in a wooden mortar with an
iron pestle.

All four of them brought in their retinue whole
battalions of Strygi or blood-suckers, of voracious
Trolls, Marowitzes, and Kikimoras, who smothered
their victims; of Polkrans and Leschyes, the latter
a kind of dwarf satyrs, who could at will change
into giants, and the former half men and half dogs,
singing and barking alternately. Their songs, as
fearful as their barkings, spread terror around them,
and they themselves killed at a hundred yards' distance by the venom of their breath.

Such were the allies whom the Roman and Scandinavian gods arrayed against Christianity.

When the new comers had been properly organ-
ized, Jupiter's eagle rose above the clouds, uttered
three piercing cries, turning to the three points of
the horizon, and at once from the East, from the
West, and from the South, there came forth the
gods of Rome and Greece, abandoning their mysterious retreats. There was Neptune with his Tritons, his Harpies, and his marine monsters; and

there was Pluto with his Fates, his Furies, and his whole host from hell.

Odin struck his buckler, and from the far North came not only the gods and the Valkyrias, with the heroes of Walhalla, but even the adversaries of the Ases, — Hela, the wolf Fenris, the Giants of the Frost with Loki at their head, — and all enlisted under him to take part in the immense slaughter.

Never had the armies of a Darius, an Alexander, an Attila, or a Charlemagne, presented a more imposing and more terrible aspect; nor has the world ever seen the like since.

When the Sibyls and the Norns, the augurs and the witches had been consulted, the march began.

A few miles from the other side of the river, in the direction of Argentoratum (Strasbourg), about half way up the slope of a gentle hill, there stood a little chapel which had not been quite finished.

The Sibyls and Druidesses had pointed out this building as the end of the first day's march, not doubting but that the god of the Christians would appear at the head of his legions, to defend his temple.

The Confederates were advancing silently under cover of the night in order to surprise the enemy, whom they thought fully prepared for resistance. Odin was in command of the right wing of the army, Jupiter of the left. The Scythian, Sarmatian, Borussian, and Finnish deities under the orders of Tabiti, Perun, Percunos, Wainamoinen, and Radgost, commanded the centre.

As soon as they came in sight of the hill, they noticed a very peculiar twinkling light, which shone out from the deep darkness, and was surrounded below by a circle of light.

Immediately the three light-footed messengers of the Roman, Slavonic, and Scandinavian gods, Mercury, Algis, and Hermode, were sent out to reconnoitre, accompanied by the Eumenides, the Valkyrias, and a small detachment of Lapithes and Centaurs. When they returned they reported that the light proceeded from the flaming swords of ten thousand destroying angels. They were quite sure of it.

Some of the allies immediately rushed forth, as is the usage in all epic battles, to challenge the chiefs of the angels to single combat. But Jupiter and Odin, thinking that all these private contests can only jeopardize the success of the great battle, compelled them to obey orders.

Thor, who had been one of the first to rush forth, was so much disappointed, that in his anger he let his heavy mace fall upon a little town that was on their route, and that might possibly have impeded the progress of the army. The mace instantly returned to the hand of the owner, and then fell and returned again and again.

Thanks to this incident, the plain had been cleared and levelled at the same time, and the signal for the attack was given at once. The Corybantes beat their drums in muffled tones; the chants of the Bards and the Skalds responded from the right and the left wing, although their harps were soon drowned in the bleat of the trumpets, the furious barking of Cerberus, the three-headed dog, of his brother dog Garm, and the howlings of the Strygi, the Kikimoras, and the Polkrans.

This was by no means all of the concert.

Mars, Odin, Potrympos, and the other war-gods now drew their swords, which produced a fearful grating sound as they came out of their sheaths; next Jupiter sounds his thunder among the Romans, and after him thunder Perun among the Slaves, Ukko among the Finns, and Thor among the Scandinavians. The repeated crash of thunder and lightning mingles with the rumbling of the chariots of Tabiti, of Flintz, the skeleton god, and of Poculos and Stribog, the gods of waterspouts and of Northern tempests; the Egipans, the Cyclops, the

blacksmiths of Ilmarinnen, begin to push immense masses of rock before them, brandishing entire oak trees as spears; while the Giants of the Frost with fearful clamor, which is taken up by the whole army of invaders, follow them, led by the equally gigantic Yaga-Baba, the terrible conductor of such an infernal concert, who marks the time by beating with his iron pestle upon his wooden mortar.

All these fearful noises, all these echoing explosions, seem to confound heaven and earth; the horizon trembles and shakes, the mountains start and stagger.

But the holy hill stands unmoved.

The light which at first shone only at the base has gradually risen as high as the summit, and the little chapel now shines brightly like a brilliant constellation.

Surprised at seeing no enemy appear, the army of the pagan gods makes a halt.

Suddenly, O miracle! lifted up as if by a gust of wind from on high, the little chapel vanishes, and in its place is seen a simple altar surmounted by a cross.

Before this altar stands a young maid, showing neither ornament nor weapon of defense, — a Virgin barefooted, with a child in her arms.

She comes down the hill, a smile on her lips; the brilliant light still encircles her brow and the brow of the infant; she comes straight up to the allied gods, who begin to look at each other in utter consternation.

She draws nearer, and all of a sudden an irresistible panic seizes Jupiter and Odin, Mars and Thor, Wainomoinen and Perun, together with the Eumenides, the Tassanis, the Cyclops, and the Giants, and all turn back towards the river, cross it in fearful disorder, and crush each other in their desperate flight, while their own temples and their own statues fall to pieces in the universal destruction.

Some of these were buried in the Rhine, where we shall hereafter find them once more; the remainder reached in sad condition their northern homes, abandoning almost the whole of Germany to Jesus and Mary.

It is but right to notice that in all the traditions which speak of this struggle between the gods and the rising religion of Christ, no mention is ever made of the Teut and the Esus of the Celts, the Alfader of the Scandinavians, the Jumala of the Finns, and the Bog of the Slaves, — nor is the Unknown God of the Romans ever mentioned. The reason is that each one of these grand deities, like the Indra of the Indian heaven, contained all the others and represented to the mind the idea of the only one eternal God.

This grand but vain effort of the pagan gods was made, according to tradition, about the year 510 of the Christian era. In the course of the same year King Clovis determined to erect a temple in honor of Christ which should be worthy of Him, and laid the foundation of the Minster at Strasbourg, perhaps with a design to replace the little chapel, which had disappeared in so miraculous a manner.

16

X.

X.

ALL who know me and esteem me will testify
to my great natural modesty. Even when I have

to do with fables, I would not venture to invent the smallest thing; I am incapable of committing such a crime. Nevertheless, some of my incredulous readers, when they see the marvelous nature of the poem, in which the triumph of Jesus and Mary over the allied pagan gods was celebrated, might possibly fancy it to be a product of my imagination. In self-defense I feel bound to quote here one of the countless traditions which allude to this great event. I once more borrow from the Muse of the Finns.

" There lived in those days a virgin who was so pure, so pure and chaste, that her eyes had never seen anything but the eyes of her sisters, that her hands had never yet touched a being in creation for the purpose of caressing it.

" She lived alone in her chamber, in company with her distaff, and ignorant of what happened even within the narrow circle of shadows which the sun traced around her house, and the image of a man was as foreign to her eyes as it was to her mind. Her thoughts and her eyes had alike kept their chastity perfect.

" She was called Marietta.

" One day, on a fine spring morning, Marietta felt a vague and incomprehensible desire to enjoy the beauties of Nature. Her heart rose within her with strange emotion.

" Impelled rather by a desire of her own than by a command from on high, she opened her door and hastened to a meadow inclosed with a hedge, which was near the house.

" In this hedge a sweet-briar was in bloom. She drew near to inhale the fragrance ; she touched the flower, and that was all that was needed. Marietta became a mother, and when her son was born she felt by the boundless pride that filled her heart, that she had given birth to a god.

" In the mean time the other gods of her own country and of the adjoining countries had been warned by their prophetesses that this child, born of a virgin and a flower, would one day drive them out of heaven ; they assembled, fully armed and determined that mother and child must both die so as to prevent the threatened catastrophe.

" At the moment when they were holding their secret councils, Marietta appeared in their midst holding her infant in her arms, and all these gods, who had until now wielded such absolute power, fled in dismay to the far North, and the icy gates of the North Pole closed behind them."

This is the story of Marietta and her child Jesus.

It would certainly seem as if this naïve account, well known among the ancient legends of Finland, was nothing less than a slight sketch of that great epic poem which we have laid before our readers.

We have only filled out the details by the aid of similar documents.

Henceforth Christianity enjoyed the results of that great day at Argentoratum. At a later period the conquered gods, it is true, showed once more signs of resistance on isolated points, but from the first, this triumph of Mary and Jesus, and perhaps also the victories obtained by King Clovis, changed the first dawn of Christianity in Germany into a kind of purifying conflagration, which spread rapidly from the Rhine to the Weser and from the Weser to the Danube.

Curious circumstances sometimes came to its assistance. Thus, many Teutons had been taught by their Druid teachers to acknowledge but one single God, and this primitive doctrine naturally reconciled them to the new creed. But, more than that, the particular god whom they thus acknowledged, was called *Esus*, almost Jesus! Others had followed the example of the Slaves and worshipped the handle of their swords, which bore the form of a cross; they naturally recognized in the Christian cross a familiar emblem of protection and safety. Even baptism was in no way distasteful to the followers of Odin. They readily adopted it in memory of the regular and regenerative ablutions with water which their ancient creed prescribed. Odin had said to them in the Runic chapter of the

Edda : " If I wish a man never to perish in combat, *I sprinkle him with water soon after his
birth.*"

Finally, this just man, put to death by wicked
men, this risen Christ, reminded them forcibly of
their own god Balder. Evidently the predicted time
had come. Balder, the ancient prisoner of Niflheim, was about to renew the world ; in his new
shape, the Bright God was no longer the son of
Frigg ; he was now Mary's son and his name was
Jesus.

This disposition, however, although plainly shown
in many parts of Germany, was by no means
unanimous.

At the table of King Clovis, the bishops, and
Saint Reni himself, were compelled to sit by the
side of Scandinavian Druids. When they intoned
their Benedicite, the latter never failed to pour out
their libations in honor of Asa-Thor and Asa-Freyr.
In spite of all the heroic and indefatigable efforts of
the priests, polytheism survived even among the new
converts, who would walk devoutly in the processions of Christian worship, while they carried their
idols and their fetishes under their arms, and who
never failed to make the sign of the cross when
they passed a tree or a spring that had been held
sacred by their forefathers. What could be done to
make them sincere and orthodox Christians ?

Liberty, in the sense in which we understand it now, and have good reason to understand it, would have appeared to a Teuton or a Slave as a beautiful woman, with a wooden yoke around her neck and all her limbs in chains. Germany had her laws, as well as every other Northern country her written or unwritten laws, but the dignity of a free-born man consisted mainly in disregarding these laws. The free man left his country, to engage in war wherever he chose, and his family, to live in any country he might prefer. It was the same thing with religious matters; he reserved to himself his independent judgment, the right to worship as he chose and the privilege of combining such articles of creed as pleased him.

This curious freedom of religion, this curious amalgamation of creeds, produced the strange result, that the neophytes especially remained half pagan and half Christian, and preferred generally to "ride on the fence" between the two creeds.

In the Nibelungen Lied, which we look upon as nothing more than a great epic poem of the Scandinavians, pagan at first but Christianized at a later period, men are represented as going devoutly to church after having consulted the Nix of the river as to their future fate. This is, no doubt, a true picture of the Germany of the early Christian days.

Some looked upon baptism, with its magnificent and pompous ceremonies, as a pleasure; others submitted to it for a consideration. Ozanam, who is exceedingly well informed about everything that refers to this curious period of transition in point of religion, tells the following anecdote: —

"One day there was a crowd of candidates for baptism; each one of them was, as usual, dressed in white, as emblematic of purity. This symbolic dress, made of a suitable material, was a present from the Church to the neophyte, which he had carefully to preserve as an evidence of his conversion. Now, on that day, all the available robes had been given away, when one more candidate for baptism presented himself; the priest found at last a robe of light color, but unfortunately in wretched condition.

"What do you mean?" exclaimed the neophyte, angrily drawing back; "have I not a right to claim a white robe as well as the others, and one of fine wool?" and looking furiously at the priest he added: "Do you think I am a man to be taken in? This is the twentieth time that I am baptized, and I have never been offered such rags before!"

The naïve candor of this good Teuton could make me almost believe that he misunderstood the nature of the ceremony altogether, and looked upon it only as a gratuitous distribution of wearing apparel.

Other more painful mistakes were made when the Christian missionaries, crossing rivers and seas at the risk of their lives, went to the uttermost confines of Germany, and there encountered half savage nations who were still worshipping the Scandinavian gods.

The patient zeal, the gentleness, and the eloquence of these holy men, succeeded finally in overcoming the convictions of these barbarians, and in introducing among them not only the Gospel, but also the worship of saints. The people received baptism, and not only welcomed the saints with great eagerness and enthusiasm, but in their desire to do them all the honor in their power, they hastened to turn every one of them into a god! They erected altars to these new gods, and on these altars they offered them human sacrifices.

These same missionaries had been instructed to prohibit the use of horseflesh among the new converts; but they found it very difficult to overcome a custom which at that time was very general.

We can hardly, at the present day, understand the importance which the Church attached to this abstinence, since now-a-days the best of people are perfectly willing to allow their horses to be taken from their stables for the purpose of being served up at table !

The most serious difficulty in all such critical periods is this, that while the true and faithful clergymen by their prodigious labors and admirable self-devotion succeeded in converting and disciplining great multitudes, false priests appeared among them, taking forcible possession of parishes and bishoprics, often without waiting till they became vacant. Pepin of Heristal and Charles Martel, his son, had just compelled the pagan Saxons to take refuge behind the Weser. When the war was over and they proceeded to dismiss the commanders of this numerous army till the beginning of another campaign, as was the custom in those days, the majority among them claimed, as a reward for services rendered, the right to exchange the sword for the crozier and the helmet for the mitre. They evidently thought that the profession was an easy one to practice and rich in rewards.

Pepin and Charles resisted, but they had to give way.

To the great disgust of the newly converted populations and to the great injury of the holy cause, which they professed to have served, these warrior-priests brought with them into the Church the manners of the camp and the fortress. They surrounded themselves with squires, falconers, and riding-masters, with horses and hounds ; they hawked, they hunted, they lived high, giving themselves up to all kinds of excesses, and drawing the sword against any one who should venture to reproach them.

When war began once more, they almost all returned to arms, without, on that account renouncing their ecclesiastic duties. Gerold, Bishop of Mayence, perished in a battle against the Saxons ; his son succeeded him on the episcopal throne, and had hardly been consecrated when he proceeded to avenge his father. He rushes into battle, challenges Gerold's murderer, kills him, and quietly returns to

Mayence for the purpose of officiating there at Mass and of returning thanks to God for his success.

Such acts of violence and such worldly enjoyments were incomprehensible to the faithful; gradually the Church of the Apostles began to fear the Church of the Soldiers. The Saxons, having vastly increased their numbers by an alliance with the Scythians and Scandinavians, appeared once more in the field.

" But," exclaims the reader, whom I fancy I hear at this distance, " but this is history, church history moreover, and you told us you would tell us all about gods ! "

I confess I did, sir; and that is the reason why I have traced out, on this historical ground, the narrowest and shortest possible path, on which I can safely return to my own domain.

" Well, then, let us return, my good friend."

I beg your pardon, sir, but before we return, allow me at least to glorify three men, who were called upon at that time to save Christianity, and with it civilization, by the pen, the word, and the sword. These equally great and equally heroic men are now three of our saints.

" Saints again ! "

Yes, sir, the first is Pope Gregory, the second Saint Boniface the missionary, and the third the Emperor Charlemagne. Do not be afraid; I shall

do no more than mention them, for fear of going
again out of my way and of speaking of forbidden
subjects, against which you have warned me. Allow me, however, to add that if the struggle which
the great Emperor undertook, was a long and terrible one, it was also glorious far beyond all. Was
it not marvelous, I ask you, to see this nation of
Franks, which but just now consisted of a mixture
of barbarians, go forth under the command of their
young king, to become the protector of Rome, of
civilization, and of Christianity? The mace had become a shield, the siege-ram a wall and a rampart.

"Of course! Everybody knows that!"

But, did you know this, sir : When the Saxons,
conquered for the tenth time, had received baptism,
together with their king Witikind, when the Rhine,
also baptized, had become a French river and a
Christian river, when the whole of Germany bowed
low before the cross, one of the nations of that
country, the Borussians (Pruszi, or Prussians), refused to give up their old gods, and continued to
refuse for several centuries to come? And yet it
was so. The proscribed gods, finding a refuge on
the banks of the Oder and the Spree, paid frequent
visits, as was quite natural, to their former followers. It was thus that the old pagan creed was
long preserved in the remote regions of Germany.
You see, sir, I have returned to my subject.

Let us rapidly conclude this first part of our task, so as to reach at last the modern gods, who were as popular as the others, and in their way neither less strange nor less curious.

During the time of the Middle Ages, Germany had been filling up with towns and castles, feudal dungeons bearing aloft a helmet and a cross. The cross arose wherever two streets met in a city and at every cross-road in the country; the most beautiful cathedrals in the world and the most magnificent monasteries were reflected in her broad river; and still, in field and forest, in city and country, and along the banks of the Rhine, the false gods were worshipped in secret.

As the church taught that they were to be looked upon as demons, the people dared not treat them badly. Demons are not guests to be turned out rudely.

"From the eighth century of our Christian era," says one of our erudite authorities, "the Saxons and Sarmatians heard the Christian missionaries speak so continually of the formidable power of Satan, that they thought it best to worship him secretly in order to disarm his wrath and perhaps to win his favor. They called him the Black God or *Tybilinus ;* the Germans call him, even now, *Dibel* or *Teufel.*"

This Black God now became for all the German

17

nations the army leader of their proscribed gods, an army which was presently to be largely increased.

The princes and knights, followed by their vassals, departed in large numbers, on the Crusades, but they brought back from the Crusades, together with holy relics, traditions of Gnomes, Peris, and Undines.

The Rhine, disgusted at the loss of his royal dignity, and determined to take his vengeance on the warrior-bishops, received these last arrivals as he had those who came before. In his healing waters the Undines mingled with the Tritons and

the Naiads; the Gnomes found shelter under the rocks, where they were hospitably received by the Dwarfs, and in the evening twilight the Nymphs, the Elves, and the Dryads danced once more merrily in company with Sylphs, Fairies, and Peris.

No doubt Christian Germany looked afterwards at all this more in the light of food for the imagination than of trouble for the conscience, but in that happy land, where people believe and dream

at the same time, and where the words of the poet
are as true as the Gospel, the imagination easily
gets the better of conscience. Thus the search
after the little blue flower led many a learned man
astray, far off into half satanic paths. Besides, it

" HAVE TRANSFERRED THEIR OLYMPUS TO THE BROCKEN."

lies in the nature of the German mind, which has
always a tendency towards idealism, its magnetic
pole, to oppose to the orthodox religion another
more secret and more mysterious creed.

This was the case already in the fourteenth and

fifteenth century; it is the case still in this, the
nineteenth century, especially among the country
people, who have passed through the age of witchcraft in which the Black God ruled supreme, and,
completely modifying their pagan notions, have
transferred their Olympus to the Brocken, the
mountain of the Witches' Sabbath.

Let us now see what the dwellers on the banks
of the Rhine have done with all their old gods
and demi-gods of every denomination.

XI.

XI.

ELEMENTARY SPIRITS OF AIR, FIRE, AND WATER. — *Sylphs, their Amusements and Domestic Arrangements. — Little Queen Mab. — Will-o'-the-Wisps. — White Elves and Black Elves. — True Causes of Natural Somnambulism. — The Wind's Betrothed. — Fire-damp. — Master Haemmerling. — The Last of the Gnomes.*

THE reader is requested to recall what I have said before, that in Germany manners, customs, and creeds, matters of prejudice as well as matters of art, and even of science, may have a beginning,

but never have an end. In that ancient home of
mysticism and of philosophy, everything is perma-
nently rooted, everything is made for eternity, like
those old oak trees of the Hercynia of antiquity:
when the parent tree is cut down, and has no longer a trunk to bear boughs and branches, it sends
forth new shoots from the roots. Druidism also has
become permanent there. We have seen it fight
against the gods of the Romans; it fought in like
manner against Christianity under Witikind; it was
kept alive, though in concealment, by the first icon-
oclasts or image breakers, and when that whole vast
country was at last conquered and became wholly
devoted to Catholicism, it broke forth once more
quite unexpectedly in the first days of the Reformation. Luther was a Druid still.

Thanks to this tenacity of life which characterizes creeds, and thanks to the prolific nature of
that soil, whatever seems to have disappeared, rises
again, under new forms, and whatever has perished
is recalled to life in some way or other. Let us
prove this.

Among all those gods which we have mentioned
before, none surely would seem to have been more
readily forgotten, swept away by the wind, which
they claimed to render useless, or buried in the
dust with which they seemed to compete, than
those tiny, microscopic deities, called Monads.

And yet this was by no means the case. Did they not, in fact, represent the elementary spirits? And the worship of the elements continued in spite of all other creeds which tried to suppress it forever.

Only these atomic deities, still quite small, exceedingly small, had increased in the most astonishing manner, when compared with their original diminutiveness. They had even assumed a form and .a body, a visible body and a shape by no means void of grace.

They had become Alps or Alfs, better known afterwards under their Eastern designation of Sylphs.

It happened occasionally that a belated traveller, a peasant or a charcoal burner, returning homeward from a wedding towards the beginning of night, would be fortunate enough to meet at a clearing in the woods or on the banks of a brook with a band of little goblins, who were making merry in the dim twilight.

These were Sylphs, a little people flying in swarms through the air, making their nest in a flower or building one with a few bits of grass at the foot of a broom-sedge, and going out only in the evening to pay visits and as good neighbors to perform their social duties.

If the traveller, the peasant, or the charcoal bur-

ner had walked softly on the fine sand of the brook
or on a grass-grown path on which his steps could
not be heard, and if he had then stopped in time

so as to be able to see without being seen, he
might witness their gambols and ascertain the secrets of their private life, without running any
risk.

Have you, dear reader, have you heard Mercutio,
in Shakespeare's " Romeo and Juliet," relate how
Queen Mab came, and say: —

" Oh, then, I see, Queen Mab hath been with you. . . . .
Her wagon spokes made of long spinners' legs,
The cover of the wings of grasshoppers,
The traces of the smallest spider's web,
The collars of the moonshine's watery beams,
Her whip of cricket's bone, the lash of film,
Her wagoner, a small, gray-coated gnat ! "

Well, the peasant, the traveller, or the charcoal
burner, enjoyed a sight which was by no means
less curious.

Some of his Sylphs, suspending a thread of gos-
samer from one blade of grass to another, made
a delightful swing for their amusement, or took a
spider's web to supply them with a hammock.
Others danced wildly about in the air, beating their
tiny wings with harmonious accuracy and furnishing thus an orchestra for the aerial ball.

Not far from them some little sylph ladies, no
doubt excellent housekeepers, were washing their
linen in the beams of the moon, or preparing a
feast.

The provisions consisted of a mixture of honey
with the nectar of flowers, a few drops of milk
which the hanging udders of young heifers had left
on the high grass, and a few pearls of that precious
dew which aromatic plants secrete ; this mixture
was used as a seasoning for some butterfly-eggs
beaten up white as snow.

If during the repast darkness fell upon them and

suddenly covered the guests with its sombre cloak, other hobgoblins, the Will-o'-the-Wisps, with wings of fire, came and took seats at the hospitable table, paying for their entertainment by diffusing a pleasant light all over the place.

The principal occupation of these elves consisted in walking before the wanderer who had lost his way so as to lead him back again into the right path.

Such were some of the harmless spirits of Air and Fire. Everything has, however, been changed in these two elements. The Will-o'-the-Wisps especially, angry at the reports of wicked people, that they are nothing more than the products of burning hydrogen, or at best phosphorus in a volatile form floating above damp places, have conceived a veritable hatred against men and now only appear when they wish to tempt travellers into marshes and deep ravines.

As to the Sylphs, they also seem to have heard similar stories which have been told about them, or they may have been irritated by the chemist Liebig, who in his " Treatise on the Composition of the Air," absolutely denies their existence, having found in his apparatus neither Sylphs nor Sylphides.

They have changed into faithless Elves, hostile to men, like the other Gnomes.

DANCE OF THE WHITE FAIRIES.

The Fairies of our day are divided into two formidable classes.

The White Fairies are damsels who wander about
on meadows and in woods, like the Willis of the
Slaves, and lie in wait for inexperienced young
men, whom they persuade to join in their dances
and keep dancing, till they lose their breath and
generally fall to the ground never to rise again.
German stories are full of such wicked tricks.
The place where they perform their diabolic
dances, becomes quite silvery under their feet.
The shepherds can thus at once recognize the
place where they have been, and are sure to hasten
away at once with their flocks.

The Black Fairies personify Nightmare and Somnambulism, but only Natural Somnambulism, it must
be borne in mind.

When men fall into this state, the Black Elf
directs all the motions of the sleeper; he lives in
him, thinks and acts for him, makes him get
upon the furniture and climb upon roofs, and keeps
him from falling, unless. . . . . Poor sleeper, be
careful! The Black
Fairies are treacherous
and cruel; the Fairy
who controls you for
the moment may at
any moment take a
fancy to throw you
from your height.

The Alfs, who have
thus become Elves or
Fairies, are of course
not the only Spirits of
the Air ; their fragile
and delicate structure
would never have al-
lowed them breath enough to swell the sails of a
vessel or to chase the clouds from one end of
the heavens to another.

Among the Celts all magicians had been able to
command the winds and the tempests at will; even
now certain men in Norway and in Lapland will
sell you, for a small price, the wind you desire to
carry you home.

In Germany, on the contrary, the wind was looked upon as an elementary power. It was not deified, as in Rome, where there was a whole windy family of gods, like Eurus, Æolus, Boreas, and Favonius, but it was an important personage, with a will of his own and independent action. The poets did their part to give im-portance to *Master Wind*.

I have in my hand a ballad, which will enable the reader to judge for himself : —

" Gretchen, the pretty miller's daughter, was courted by the son of the king. Her father, the miller, knowing that kings' sons are not apt to marry, had chosen her a husband, a young flour merchant from Rotterdam.

" The Dutchman was on his way up the Rhine ; that very evening he was expected to arrive, to make his proposals.

" Gretchen called upon Master Wind to help her ; he came in by the window, but not without breaking a number of panes.

" ' What do you wish me to do ? '

" ' A man wants to marry me, against my will; he is coming in a sail boat ; contrive it so that he cannot land at Bingen.'

" The wind blew, and blew so well that the boat, instead of coming up to Bingen, was driven back again as far as Rotterdam.

18

" At Rotterdam also it could not make land; it was driven into the North Sea, and there the Dutchman is perhaps still sailing about at this day.

" But Master Wind had made his conditions before he went to work blowing so well ; and the pretty miller's daughter had agreed to them without hearing them, for all around her the furniture, the doors, and the blinds were shaking and rattling furiously, thanks to her visitor. Thus it came about that poor Gretchen found herself betrothed to Master Wind, which made her very sad, for now she had less hope than ever of marrying the king's son.

" However, Master Wind was as gallant towards his fair betrothed as he could be. Every morning, when she opened her window, he would throw her in beautiful bouquets of flowers which he had torn off in the neighboring gardens.

" If any young man of the village, whom she had rejected, passed without saluting her, Master Wind was promptly at hand to carry off his hat and send it up in the air so high, that soon it looked no bigger than a lark. It was well for him that Master Wind did not, with the hat, take his head off at the same time.

" One day (when Master Wind must have been asleep), the king's son came to the mill, made his way without difficulty to Gretchen's chamber, and forthwith desired to kiss her. Gretchen did not object. But at once, and although out of doors all was quiet, the tables and chairs performed a wild dance, and the doors and· windows began to slam as if they had been mad.

"Gretchen herself began to twirl around and around in the most unaccountable manner; her hair was loosened by an invisible hand and whisked about her head with strange rustling and dismal whistling.

"Terrified by the sight of a tempest in a close room, the prince cried: —

"'Ah! accursed one, you are the betrothed of Master Wind!'

"And at the same moment a terrible gust of wind carried off the king's son, the miller's daughter, and the mill, and no one ever saw or heard anything more of them.

"Perhaps they went to join the Dutchman, who was all the time sailing about in the North Sea, or the hat, which was still on its way in the clouds."

The legend does not tell us whether it was before or after this occurrence that Master Wind married Mistress Rain.

So much for the Spirits of the Air.

As for the Spirits of the Fire, it must be re-

membered that the Will-o'-the-Wisps were by no
means their only representatives. There were also
Salamanders, too well known to be described here;
and St. Elmo Fires, near relations of the Will-o'-
the-Wisps. But we must pause a moment to speak
of the formidable Fire-damp, the miner's terror.
The remarkable feature about it is that it plays so
insignificant a part in the popular German myths,
although it has destroyed so many victims in all
mountainous countries, and above all in the Hartz
mountains.

This subterranean lightning, far more fatal than
that of the upper regions, is known to the people
of the Rhine simply as a tall monk, whom they
call Master Haemmerling.

Master Haemmerling visits the mines from time
to time in the guise of a harmless amateur, or of
an inspector, who is not fond of being hurried.
However, on Fridays especially, he is subject to
violent attacks of anger. If a laborer handles his
pickaxe awkwardly, or if he is insolent to his master, or the master harsh to him and requiring too
much, he is, quick as a flash of lightning, between
them when they are as yet half way under ground.
Then he suddenly draws his long legs together,
and between his two knees crushes their heads with
as little hesitation and ceremony as a mother would
show in destroying between her two thumbs the

little hateful insect that has troubled her darling child.

Nothing more need be said of the elementary spirits of Air and Fire; but as we have followed Master Haemmerling into the lower depths of the mountains, we might just as well remain there a while and make the acquaintance of the Gnomes, the Spirits of the Earth.

Can you see, through the dense air which fills these immense caverns, the long, gigantic stalactites, reaching from the ceiling to the floor and strongly impregnated with iron ? They are the columns of this subterranean palace, and around these stalactites, peaceful, slumbering waters form a kind of little lakes, the shores of which look as if they were covered with rust.

Here and there, in the damp low grounds, half choked with ore and slag of various kinds, dark reeds are growing in the shape of lizards ; like lizards they bend backwards, moving their heads from side to side and showing thus the diamond eye which shines brilliantly at the extreme end.

These dark depths seem to teem with fantastic creatures ; close by a heap of grains of gold, stands immovable a watchful, silent guardian, a griffin ; a pack of black dogs, also guardians of the treasures hid in this world of precious metals and

stones, are roaming incessantly along the ceiling.
On the sloping sides, dwarfs not larger than grasshoppers, and jumping about like peas in the sieve
of the winnower, are gathering right and left the
tiny gold and silver spangles which are left at their
disposal, while enormous toads are posted about as
watchmen.

Finally, far back in the remotest part of these
abysses the kings of this empire are moving about;
these thick-set men, with stout limbs and monstrous heads, are the Gnomes.

But people hardly believe in Gnomes any longer;
the hard-working miners who ought to come every
day in contact with them, deny their existence, and
they have gradually passed into the class of fabu-
lous beings.

Still, I am told that as recently as last year, a
pretty peasant girl from the neighborhood of Ham-
burg appeared on a certain evening at a ball, with
a large ruby on her finger. She professed to have
received this gem from an Earth Spirit, who had
appeared to her at the entrance to the Faunus
mines.

The gossips of the village were not satisfied,
however, with the account, and suspected the
Gnome to have been an English Gnome, who
was travelling abroad for his health and courting
pretty girls for his amusement. This conviction

was so strong that the poor girl had to leave the country in disgrace.

This is the last Gnome that has been mentioned in that part of Germany.

XII.

XII.

" AFTER leaving Aix-la-Chapelle, I had stopped at Cologne, on the left bank of the Rhine, which I then found completely covered with several rows of women, a countless and charming multitude. . . . . Adorned with flowers or aromatic herbs, the sleeves pushed up above the elbow, they dipped their soft white hands and arms into the river, murmuring certain mysterious words which I could not understand.

" I questioned some people. They told me it was an ancient custom of the country. Thanks to these ablutions and certain prayers which accompanied them, the river carried down with it all the diseases, which would otherwise have attacked them during the coming year. I answered, smilingly : ' How happy the people of the Rhine must be if the kind river thus takes all their sufferings to distant countries ! The Po or the Tiber have never been able to do as much for us.' "

These are the words which Petrarch wrote in one of his familiar letters, written on St. John's Eve.

This letter, as precious by its date as by its contents, proves beyond all question, that in the fourteenth century the Rhine was popularly worshipped and adored on the very days on which the summer solstice is celebrated by bonfires after the manner of the old fire worshippers.

Unfortunately the Christians ended by appealing to the elements, to Fire or Water, as to a judicial authority.

The popular notion that the elements were perfectly pure and would hence instinctively reject every impure substance, led naturally to ordeals by water. The accused was undressed; his hands and feet were tied crosswise, the right hand to the left foot and the right foot to the left hand, and thus bound he was thrown into a river or any watercourse that was deep enough. If he floated, he was guilty and instantly burnt; if he sank and remained for some time at the bottom of the water, he was considered innocent — but he was drowned.

Heinrich Heine, at least, tells us that this was the infallible result of justice in the Middle Ages, and the Middle Ages ended in Germany but yesterday.

There was also a trial by bread and cheese (*exorcismus panis hordeacei, vel casei, ad probationem veri*), but bread and cheese are not elements. Let us return to the elementary spirits of Water.

During the great religious reaction which took place after the days of Charlemagne, all the mythological gods of rivers and streams had gradually returned, more or less successfully, to their former occupations. The great Nix or Nichus, upon whom devolved the rule over all the rivers of Germany, was no other than the ancient Niord, a very important deity and a kind of Northern Neptune. This very weighty discovery is due to the learned Mallet.

No doubt this god Niord was one of those who, on their disastrous flight from Argentoratum, had fallen into the Rhine. They thought that he was drowned, but he had only taken refuge in one of the lowest, almost unfathomable depths of the river. From this safe retreat the great Nichus had defied the decrees of Councils and the anathemas of the Christians hurled against all elementary spirits alike; there he had summoned the subaltern deities of sources, ponds, lakes, and smaller streams, the nymphs of the banks, and the hideous, scaly monsters which swarmed at the bottom of the river. Organizing all these into a people, an escort, and an army, he had come forth and invaded at the head of his host the banks of the Neckar and the Main, the Moselle and the Meuse, the great tributaries of the Rhine, and governed the inhabitants of the banks by terror. More than once he had extended his ravages far beyond the plains, overthrowing churches that had but just been completed, and drowning in his waters all the deserters from the altars of Odin.

Niord was a wicked god, who had a fearful temper. He held his subjects, to whatever class they might belong, completely under his yoke, treating them capriciously and cruelly, and making of the Rhine a hell of waters.

It is to this dark and damp kingdom of the great Nichus that we have to go in order to make the acquaintance, not of his great dignitaries, but of the very humblest and lowest of his subjects, the Nixen and the male and female Undines, a race of anathematized demons, who make up, by themselves, almost the whole population of this realm beneath the waters of the Rhine.

What! Must we really count our beautiful Lore, the charming fairy Lorelei, you who preferred death to the punishment of making all men fall in love with you, much as you loved men in general, must we count you among the demons, evildoing and accursed sprites? No! How public opinion has stoutly held its own in defiance of all the decrees of the Church. Nixen, like the Fairies, are by common consent divided into two classes: Nixen proper, who are former pagan deities and not too much to be dreaded, and female Nixen, almost always harmless and at times even useful.

It is these latter only of whom we shall hereafter speak as Undines..

The Nixen of the first class are ever ready to assume any disguise that may aid them in attaining their purpose. Some of them roam about in deserted places near the banks of rivers; others have at times appeared in the neighboring towns, pretending to be foreign ladies of distinction, or artists, generally great performers on the harp. Here they have begun intrigues with credulous lovers or unlucky admirers. Others appear at village celebrations, mingling in the dance with such energy, that their partners are intoxicated, carried away, and, losing their heads, think they continue to hear the sound of harps and violins, while they are already far away, led on by imaginary music, and only return to consciousness on the banks of the river, at the moment when they are about to sink helpless into the waters of the Rhine.

One important point, however, must not be overlooked. To protect one's self against the allurements of these accursed fairies, a bit of horehound or marjoram is sufficient. We hope all who propose visiting the Rhine will be careful always to keep such an herb on their person. Before they take out their passports they ought always to pay a visit to an herbalist.

The second class of Nixen, the only one in which we are interested, the Undines, are, as far as I have been able to learn, the restless souls of poor girls who, driven to despair by love, have thrown themselves into the Rhine. Unfortunately German lovers, not very courageous at best, are but too apt to seek relief in suicide.

THE NIX WITH THE HARP.

According to the somewhat uncertain information for which I am indebted to my authorities or to my intercourse with the Rosahl family, the Undines

19

are born as human beings and very inferior in power to the genuine Nixen. They live under the water exactly the same time they would have lived on earth, if they had not voluntarily put an end to their existence. They are thus granted a kind of exceptional resurrection and have here a preliminary purgatory, in which they but too frequently expiate, if not the sin of their love, at least that of their death.

In the lowest depths of the river, at the bottom of vast, submerged grottoes, a secret tribunal, presided over by the great Nichus, holds its solemn meetings. Here they are disciplined with the utmost severity, as is abundantly proven by a great number of terrible stories, such as the account of the three Undines of Sinzheim, which the two brothers Grimm report in their great work.

Three young girls of marvelous beauty, three sisters, appeared every evening at the social meetings of Epfenbach, near Sinzheim and took their seats among the linen-spinners. They brought new songs and merry stories which no one had heard before. Where did they come from ? No one knew, and no one dared to ask for fear of appearing suspicious. They were the delight of these meetings, but as soon as the clock struck ten they rose, and neither prayers nor supplications could induce them to stay a moment longer.

One evening the schoolmaster's son, who had fallen in love with one of them, undertook to prevent their departure at the usual hour ; he put back the wooden clock, which usually gave them warning.

The next day some people from Sinzheim, who were walking by the side of the lake, heard groans

rising from the depths of the lake, while the surface was stained by three large spots of blood. From that time the three sisters were never seen again at the evening assemblies, and the schoolmaster's son faded away gradually. He died very soon afterwards.

These three sisters, so gentle, so lovely and laborious, had in nothing betrayed a connection with the spirits of the lower world. The only thing was, that people remembered how the hems of their garments had frequently been wet, a sure sign by which Undines can be recognized. Otherwise they seem to have been very much like other girls, and the severity of the great Nichus appears hardly reasonable.

As to this hour of ten o'clock, however, military rules cannot be more rigorous than his.

It must, on the other hand, not be imagined that all Undines are as gentle and resigned as these three sisters. There are some who bitterly resent having been abandoned by their lovers, and try to revenge themselves; these seem to partake to some degree of the character of the Nixen, or rather, — why should we not say so at once and quite candidly? — they remain faithful to their instincts as women.

As a proof of this statement I will quote a short but perfect little drama, which Miss Margaret Rosahl has, at my request, copied from Busching's voluminous collection.

Count Herman von Filsen, whose estates lay on the right bank of the Rhine, between Oslerspey

and Brauback, was about to marry the rich heir-
ess of the castle of Rheins, on the other bank.
His messenger had started to carry the letters
of invitation to all the guests, but a sudden rise of
the waters had nearly prevented his crossing a small
stream. In trying to get over, his horse stumbled,
and was drowned. The messenger, however, did
not lose courage, but went on his way on foot.
Everywhere he found the brooks swollen into
streams, and the torrent seemed to press him more
and more closely, describing curves and zigzags,
with countless cataracts, barring him the way on
all sides and making the usual path impassable.

By the aid of a huge stick and jumping from
rock to rock, the poor, half bewildered man kept
on, walking well-nigh at hap-hazard, till he found
himself near the Rhine, into which the swollen torrent, rushing after him with sudden fury, seemed
determined to push him.

Fortunately a small boat was lying quite near
the shore: he loosened it, took the oars, and returned to Filsen.

When he reached the castle he said to the
Count: "Sir, a Nix has barred me the way."

The Count did not believe in Nixen. He sent
out another messenger. But the same adventure
befell him.

The wedding day had been fixed and the Count

went on, although he feared his friends and followers would be few in number.

One morning, as he crossed the river from the
right bank to the left, in order to pay a visit to
his lady love, a sudden tempest broke out. He
thought he saw a pale form arise from the waters,
bending over the bow of the boat and trying to

draw it down into the abyss beneath the waters.
Thereupon he became thoughtful, sent for his
steward, and ordered him to find out what had become of a certain girl of the neighborhood, Gottfriede from Braubach.

"I met her a few days ago," replied the steward, "as she was going to St. Mark's Chapel, and I offered her holy water. Gottfriede asked me about your approaching wedding. She was very well, and seemed to be in good spirits."

"Go and see if you can find her," said the Count, "and bring me word."

During the wedding feast Hermann von Filsen appeared joyous and attentive to his bride, the new Countess, but the effort to appear so caused his perspiration to break out profusely, especially when

all of a sudden a small woman's foot, white and delicate, appeared to his eyes, and to his only, on the ceiling of the dinner-hall.

He felt a chill in all his limbs. He rose suddenly and fled to another room, followed by his wife, his mother, and all the guests, who thought he had been seized with sudden illness.

In this room he saw, and he alone again saw, a white hand raise a curtain and with the forefinger beckon him to follow.

Long time ago Hermann had heard, without paying any attention at that time to the statement, that such a small white foot and a small white hand indicated the presence of an Undine and the coming of an inevitable calamity.

Now he believed it.

The bishop, who had performed the marriage ceremony, was at the dinner. Hermann went straight up to him, knelt down, and confessed aloud, and with many tears, that a young girl named Gottfriede, fairer and better than all her sisters, had loved him dearly, and that he had returned her love and then abandoned her. Gottfriede had sought oblivion of her sufferings in the river, and now was bent upon revenge.

" Bless me, father, for I am going to die ! "

The bishop, before uttering the words of absolution, demanded first that the Count should abjure his impious faith in such supernatural beings, of whom the Church knew nothing.

" How can I refuse to believe what I see ? There she is ! Looking as pale as she was this morning at the bow of the boat. Her hair, full of green grass, is hanging in disorder all over her shoulders; she looks at me with a tearful smile."

"Nothing but visions!" replies the bishop. "Your eyes deceive you."

"But it is not only by the eye that I am aware of her presence, I hear her voice; she is calling me? Forgive me, Gottfriede!"

"You are out of your mind! These are the devil's snares! And who tells you that the girl has ceased to live? That she has committed a crime? Thanks be to God, Gottfriede came to me, she confessed to me penitently, and now she is in a convent!"

At this moment the assembly, already deeply excited, was somewhat startled by the entrance of the steward, who looked terrified, went up to the Count's mother, and whispered some words into her ear. She could not repress a cry.

"Dead!" she said.

"Yes, she is dead, and I also must die!" cried Hermann in accents of despair.

The young bride, offended at this avowal of a previous attachment, had at first stood aloof; now, consulting her own heart alone, she thought of contesting the right of this invisible rival, and with open arms drew near the Count; but he pushed her aside rudely.

The bishop began his exorcisms. While he was repeating the prescribed words, the Count asked: —

"What do you want of me, Gottfriede? Forgive me and we will all pray for you. You are weeping and kissing me by turns, but your kisses are nothing but bitterness and sorrow to me, since I have given my name to another, since another is my " —

He could not complete the sentence. Uttering a sharp cry he fell at full length to the ground, and on his neck appeared a long, bluish mark, such as is seen in strangled persons.

The great Nichus is, as we have seen, the master, the despot, the *Wassermann*, par excellence, of all this watery, dark world, peopled by Nixen and Undines. His authority is, moreover, by no means limited to the exercise of judicial functions; his will, constantly under the influence of an ill-regulated appetite, is law for everybody; the male Nixen are his Court, and his harem is kept full by the fairest among those women who become his own by suicide. This greenish-complexioned Sardanapalus is said to celebrate incredibly monstrous orgies with his drowned Odalisques.

He is, in reality, Niord, the Scandinavian god,

and this Niord again is, originally, one of those old Roman emperors, who were deified, and whose portraits Petronius has left us drawn in mud and blood.

His principal agent, and the Jack-of-all-trades of the whole community, Nixcobt, the messenger of the dead, has to maintain communication between the people who live on the river, and those who live in it. He is perhaps the most eccentric of all the mythical personages of the Rhine.

When morning is about to dawn and the mountain tops are beginning to glow in a faint subdued light, a kind of low, thickset man of the most hideous appearance, may occasionally be seen gliding along the houses of a town, keeping carefully in the shade, or slipping down the hill-side between the long rows of grapes, which are almost as high as he is. His terrible head turns upon his slender neck as upon a pivot, and thus he can see and examine everything without stopping for a moment. His bare shoulders, his elbows, knees, and cheekbones are covered with scales ; small pins appear

at intervals at his ankles; his round glamous eyes
have a bright red point in the centre; his teeth
and hair are green, and his enormous mouth, split
wide open and shaped like the mouth of a fish,

wears a fixed smile, which strikes terror in the be-
holder. This creature is Nixcobt.

With daybreak he is back in the river to inquire
if its mournful population has been added to over
night by some victim, suicide or not. He takes
down a description of each one, draws up a report,
inquires as to what induced them to seek refuge
in the new world, and offers them his services for
the purpose of letting the friends and parents know,

whom they may have left behind, ignorant of their fate and inconsolable at their loss.

Then he amuses the great Nichus with all his stories and all the clever tricks he has been playing during his nocturnal visits to the people in the villages and towns on the river.

These merry tricks of Master Nixcobt form even in our day an ever welcome staple of amusement to the young spinners during the long winter nights, accompanied as they are by the cheerful hum of the swiftly turning wheels.

One day Nixcobt calls upon the tax collector of a little town on the Rhine, whom he finds in great consternation. His wife has left his house and he does not know what has become of her. To console him Nixcobt tells him that she is dead, having drowned herself, and as a proof of it, he shows him a letter which he has with his own hands taken from the pockets of the deceased.

The husband, whose tears had been flowing freely, dries them quickly, becomes furious, and looks at his children with fierce glances. He is jealous of their dead mother. Nixcobt laughs and goes to some one else.

That some one else, an honest vintner of the Rheingau, has the night before killed his friend in an excess of passion and then thrown the body into the Rhine, together with the knife with which

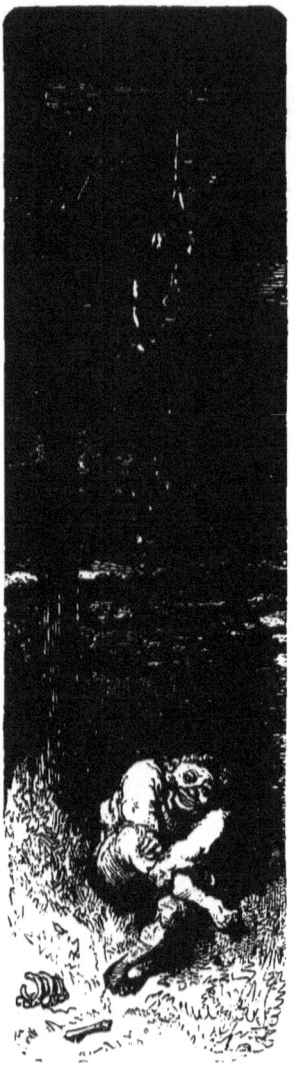

he had committed the murder. This knife Nixcobt now presents to him, for he takes delight in restoring lost objects of this kind.

While the murderer stands petrified at the sight of the still bloody knife, the Gnome hastens to the Mayor to report to him the whole matter.

An inquiry is held, the vintner is found, holding the bloody knife in his hand, he is hanged and Nixcobt laughs heartily.

One night a notary of Badenheim, near Mayence, hears in his sleep a voice saying: —

"John Harnisch, the great Nichus is courting your wife, who has been changed into an Undine three months ago; she will not listen to him, and he wants you to tell him how he must manage to please her."

The notary thought it was a bad dream, uttered a sigh as he thought of his deceased wife, and fell asleep once more. But a chilly hand resting upon his breast waked him once more, and the voice said : —

" John Harnisch, speak, speak promptly and be sincere, or you shall never sleep again."

John Harnisch resisted for some time longer, but a red flame dimly lighted up his alcove and he saw a row of green teeth and scaly cheek bones. Thoroughly frightened, he said what he could.

" Thanks ! " cries Nixcobt, and breaks out into a far sounding laugh.

We might fill folios with all the lugubrious jokes of this messenger of the dead, but we will abstain. Besides, Nixcobt has lost all respect now-a-days. He is no longer seen gliding along the houses in towns or slipping through the rows in the vine-yards.

We might in like manner tell a vast number of interesting stories and quote endless *Lieder* and ballads, which treat of Nixen and Undines. For there are, besides, Undines of rivers and Undines of lakes, and there are even some in the ocean ; in Germany all watercourses, down to the tiniest rills, have their Undines.

Only day before yesterday I was walking on the
banks of the Rhine; only yesterday on those of the
Moselle. This morning, wandering about at hap-
hazard I encountered a brook, a mere rill, which
attracted me by its sweet murmurs. I followed it,
followed it for two hours. I happened to have
nothing else to do.

My tiny rill, a mere infant so near its source,
was turning and twisting in the thick grass and
seemed to try and walk on all fours as little children do. Farther down it had become a little girl,
having increased in size and bulk; it now wandered
hither and thither, carelessly, capriciously, leaping
merrily over the rocks and carrying off here a
flower and there a flower that grew on its banks,
no doubt for the purpose of making a bouquet.
Still farther on, I witnessed its marriage with a big
brook that had come down all the way from the
mountains; it was a young woman now, a wife,
and walked soberly through the plain, like a prudent stream, bearing already boats on its surface
and preparing to join an elder sister, the Moselle.
Soon I had to cross it on a bridge; on this same
bridge four Prussian soldiers were busy watching
the water as it flowed by, no doubt in the hope of
catching a fair Undine as she was stealthily slipping down the river. As for myself, I had in vain
traced the unknown little river from its birth all

along its banks, under the thick shelter of willows and alder bushes; neither day before yesterday on the Rhine, nor yesterday on the Moselle, nor to-day, did I ever find a trace of a Nymph, a Nix, or an Undine!

What must be my conclusion?

A thief who had been brought before a police court and was there confronted with two persons who had seen him steal, said : —

" These men claim that they have seen me, but I, I could bring twenty other witnesses who would swear that they have not seen me ! "

" What does that prove ? " asked the judge of the court.

I saw nothing. " What does that prove ? " as the wise judge said to the thief.

XIII.

XIII.

FAMILIAR SPIRITS. — *Butzemann.* — *The Good Frau Holle.* — KO-
BOLDS. — *A Kobold in the Cook's Employ.* — *Zotterais and the
Little White Ladies.* — THE KILLECROFFS, *the Devil's Children.*
— *White Angels.* — GRANTED WISHES, *a Fable.*

FRANCE, which is skeptic to the core, has no idea
of the importance of certain visible or invisible
spirits, who eagerly seek the society of man, sleep-

ing under his roof, or in certain cases becoming members of his family, in the strictest sense of the word. Besides, they render efficient services to a good housekeeper; they may do great harm if they are made angry, and they give at times most useful advice.

These hobgoblins, little known outside of Germany and England, frequent also the French provinces watered by the Meuse, the Moselle, and the Rhine, and are sometimes brought to Paris by cooks from Alsace and coachmen from Lorraine.

Let us rapidly glance, not at all, but at some of the best authenticated among these familiar spirits.

Evening has come, the night is dark, and master and mistress are fast asleep. A servant with a candle in her hand and gaping to her heart's content, goes once more over the house, looking in all the corners and out of the way places and putting everything in order. All of a sudden a door is swiftly opened and closed again right in her face and her light is blown out. You will say a window has been left open and the draught has done all this.

By no means! It is the *Butzemann.*

Some merry companions are assembled in the large dining-room of the hotel and celebrate there a feast of grapes in memory of the divine Dionysius. The night advances and there they are still,

glass in hand, singing, drinking. . . . . Silence! all
of a sudden singing and drinking comes to an end;
the glasses halt half way in the midst of a toast;
the heavy eyes open wide, the trembling knees
grow strong once more. Every one of the guests
hastens home. Three times a hairy, ill-shapen crea-
ture has come and knocked with its wings against
the window. You will say it was a bat.

By no means! It is the *Butzemann!*

The family is gathering around the warm porce-
lain stove, where they can safely defy cold winter.
The men are smoking, a pot of beer by their side;
the women are knitting and talking of the approaching wedding of the eldest daughter. Oh
misery! Away back in the fireplace, a great noise
is heard; a bright light shines. Coals and sparks
are scattered all around, and some have fallen upon
the dress of the betrothed. What is the matter?
You will say again, it was a knot in the wood, perhaps a chestnut that had been overlooked in the
ashes and has burst now.

By no means! it is the *Butzemann!*

The Butzemann, a prophetic family spirit, warns
you of coming danger and bids you prepare for
an approaching misfortune. Never undertake a
journey, never get married if a clear sign has made
you aware that Butzemann has put his veto upon
your journey or your marriage. The only difficulty

you will have is to distinguish between Butzemann and a puff of wind, a bat, or an exploding chestnut.

It is much easier to recognize *Frau Holle*, as her presence is always announced by unmistakable indications. She has assumed the task of overlooking the poor country girls at their work. But it has never been found out why this benevolent fairy of work-people does not live in some great industrial city, or some beautiful country district, where the signs of active life are abundant and the whirring of wheels or the stamping of machinery is heard ; where the spinners sing, and the washerwomen beat time at the limpid stream. She prefers, with unaccountable perverseness, to live in dismal swamps, beside faithless Will-o'-the-Wisps and low Nixen !

No one has ever dared examine this question so closely as to ascertain the precise truth.

Some have dropped timid hints that Frau Holle, now occupying a very humble position and rated among the familiar spirits only, was once upon a time a high and mighty personage, but they have had nothing more to say of her past glory, as is the case with poor ladies who have been " unfortunate."

Others, with more boldness or more knowledge, have recognized in her the goddess Frigg, Odin's wife. Dear Frau Holle ! what a coming down ! what poor creatures we are, after all.

As soon as the cross was planted on the banks of the Rhine and the Danube, Frigg, under the name of Hertha (Mother Earth), had taken refuge on an island in the ocean, where she lived invisible and alone in the heart of a sacred forest, which was constantly invaded by the waves of the sea.

A priest, who had remained faithful to the old religion, alone knew the hour and the minute when the goddess would deign once more to appear to men. At the given moment he drew forth, on the marshy island, a chariot wrapped in veils. Hertha got in, and for some days travelled through the world, diffusing all around her good will and consolation. Then all wars were suspended; not only the sword went back into its sheath, but all irons, all defensive and offensive weapons and even the iron shoes of the ploughs, had to be kept carefully concealed. Hertha invited the world to enjoy peace and repose.

Now let us see in what respect Frau Holle or Holla reminds us of the good goddess.

At certain periods of the year, especially at Christmas, Frau Holle leaves her marshy island in order to inspect the world. All who work in linen, spinning, weaving, embroidery, or starching, are by turns visited by the good lady. Their idleness and their carelessness are severely punished. If one fine morning Annie finds her wheel or Kate her loom covered with green slime, if Bertha notices her work torn in the place which she repaired only the night before, or if the water has over night turned greasy and looks discolored, the poor girls may be sure that Frau Holle has been on her round of inspection.

If she is pleased, on the other hand, the ribbon around the distaff holds a pretty marshflower, a lily, an iris, or a gladiolus; on the lace cushion or on the seamstress's work a little golden needle is stuck, and on the heap of specially well washed and well folded linen lies a cake of perfumed soap, which fills the whole house with its sweet odor.

Sometimes Frau Holle finds her way mysteriously to a garret, where a poor woman is lying sick with fever, the result of overwork. Then she finishes herself the work that had been begun, and when she leaves she puts a few florins under the pillow of the sleeping sufferer.

Blessings be upon you, good Dame Holle! Even if you were really once a goddess of the first rank, you need not blush at your present condition. Still, we cannot help asking, with a slight tremor of fear, how it can have come about, that the noble Frigg, the all powerful Hertha, should have been reduced to play the lady patroness of washerwomen and seamstresses? How has this island in the ocean, with its sacred forest, become a wretched marsh, fetid and ill reputed? There is but one answer to such a question: Frigg has been unfortunate.

But the spinners and seamstresses, the clear-starchers and embroiderers are not the only ones who are honored by kind attentions from the supernatural world. The brothers Grimm say:—

" In certain parts of the world, every person — man, woman, or child — has his own goblin to do menial service; he carries water, cuts wood, and fetches beer." During all this time the master has nothing to do but to set still and to see the work done.

This goblin is evidently the *Genius loci* of the ancients.

Among all these goblins, however, one is by far the most famous in Germany, and at the same time the oddest, of whom the most extraordinary stories are told. They call him *Kobold.*

During the night the Kobold sets everything to

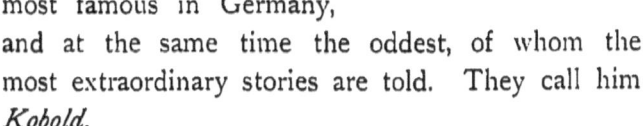

rights in the kitchen; he cleans the glasses, the plates, the pans, and wages war against the spiders and the mice. For all these attentions he asks only a little food, specially prepared for him, for he would never dream to ask for a share of his master's dinner.

Although he seems to be specially devoted to the cook's department, the Kobold is first of all attached to the house. If the cook is dismissed, or if the master moves, he nevertheless remains in his old home, quite ready to offer his services to the new comers. If the cook goes, she says to her who takes her place: —

"Do not forget to put a little panada on the kneading trough for the Kobold, or he might play you some ugly tricks. Be careful, for he is not always in good humor."

If the Kobold, or in his place the cat, eats the panada, the new cook is sure to say: —

"Chim has been here; I see we shall be good friends."

But if Chim has left the dainty untouched, or has merely tasted it, she is troubled.

"Perhaps he wants it made with the yolk of an egg? Or perhaps I had not put enough butter to it?"

Although the Kobold is almost always invisible, he is at all times ready for a chat.

What are we to make of these strange beings, the servants of our servants, who are even more faithful than the latter to the house which they have once made their home, who do not, as we are told is the case in some countries, insist so strongly upon certain privileges that it becomes uncertain whether the servants are not themselves masters and those who think themselves to be masters are in reality servants? They generally do nothing but kindness. Nevertheless they keep out of sight, thus shunning all public return for their benevolent services. What are we to make of such servants? Martin Luther answers in his " Table Talk."

" For many years," he says, " a servant had a familiar spirit who sat down by her on the hearth, where she had made a little place for him, and they talked to each other during the long winter evenings. One day she asked Heinzchen (Chim, Heinzchen, and Kurt Chimgen are the pet names by which German and Alsatian cooks generally call their Kobolds) to let her see him in his natural shape. At first Heinzchen refused,

but at last, as she insisted, he told her to go down into the cellar, where he would show himself to her." "She took a candle," he goes on to say, "and went into the cellar, where the Kobold appeared to her in the likeness of a child of hers who had died some years before. Whether he vanished then, leaving her in amazement and terror, or whether he resumed the shape in which she had been accustomed to see him, we are not told. It is a grim story upon which we do not care to dwell, for we prefer to remember the Kobold as a cheerful household companion. It is pleasant to think of those quaint little creatures, whose world is the kitchen, and to imagine the joy they feel in sharing the busy, bustling life that goes on there daily. Be sure they know every nook and corner about, — every stew-pan and ladle, and are learned in the steamy scents and fragrant savors which are the atmosphere of their home. At night when the fires are out, and the family is asleep, they have a life of their own. They are on the best possible terms with the cat, which they permit to share their food, and with which they no doubt waltz when in a gamesome mood. Happy Kobolds.

According to general belief the Kobolds belong as much to the race of men as to the world of spirits; they retain the size and shape of infants, and that knife which so often is noticed in the form of a caudal appendage, is nothing less than the instrument with which they have been put to death.

There exist, however, quite a number of troublesome hobgoblins, who turn the house upside down and deprive the people to whom they bear a grudge of all peace and sleep, till they well nigh drive them mad. But these creatures ought, in my opinion, not be mixed up with the Kobolds. The latter are almost invariably gentle and inoffensive ; if they sometimes become angry, they act just like children ; they break and smash things, but they are easily pacified by the sight of some little tit-bit, as for instance, a panada made with butter and eggs.

The Zotterais and the Little White Ladies seem, in their habits at least, to come nearer to Kobolds. Very useful and easily satisfied, the Zotterais are as fond of stables as the Kobolds are of kitchens ; they curry the horses, nurse them when they are sick, and keep everything in excellent order in their racks as well as in the harness-room.

The Little White Ladies, on the other hand, are more delicate in their instincts and often quite fastidious ; they like only blood horses, Arab or Turkish horses, and hence the popular idea that they have originated in the East.

They slip into the stables of wealthy people, while the grooms are asleep ; here they light a small candle, which they always keep about them, and then proceed to business.

In the morning, when the head coachman makes his round to see that everything is right, he sometimes finds a drop of wax on the smooth coat of a sorrel or an Isabel colored horse, and then he says to the grooms : —

" You have not had much to do to-day, my friends, with your horses ; I see the little lady has been here."

The Zotterais are of unmistakable German origin, for they take care of horses without regard to race and without the help of a wax candle. They have, of course, harder work to do and are more apt to become soiled or to have accidents ; but, nevertheless, they accomplish their purpose. They are naturally easily tired, and hence they require a knot to be made in the mane of a horse, where they can suspend themselves and rest. There is not a peasant on the banks of the Rhine or the Meuse, who would neglect this duty, and I have myself often seen them attend to it carefully.

Formerly the Zotterais also protected sheep against ticks and kept their wool from getting tangled; they even derived their name from Zotte, which means a flock of wool. In those days, it must be presumed, from the habits of those benevolent little people, the fleeces must have been whiter and better kept than they are now-a-days; but sheep raisers had the unlucky idea, produced probably by avarice, that not a particle of wool should be left on ram or ewe, and thus deprived their tiny friends of all means to rest and recover breath when hard at work. The Zotterais looked upon this neglect of what was due to them as an insult, and abandoned the flocks of sheep for the horses in the stables. Besides, they found it impossible to live on good terms with the shepherds' dogs.

We must finally mention the most important and most extraordinary of all familiar spirits, whom we must needs include among these favored beings, as he represents nothing less than the son of the house, the child of the family.

This is the *Killecroff* or *Suppositus.* [handwritten note]

The last mentioned name is given to him because this so-called son of the house is in reality

a changeling, a *supposed* child, which has been put into the place of the real child.

Who has taken the legitimate child from its cradle in order to put into its place a *Killecroff*, and who is the real father of the latter?

Both of these questions are met by one and the same answer. The Devil!

We have so far carefully avoided touching on matters of witchcraft; but unfortunately they are as well known on the banks of the Rhine as on those of the Thames and the Seine. The *Killecroffs*, however, children of the Devil and begotten according to popular belief during the orgies of the Witches' Sabbath, have been really in existence upon earth; *suppositi* or not, they have played their part in the world's history and occasionally even left behind them illustrious descendants.

In the same way as the Swedish king Vilkins and Merovæus, king of the Franks, boasted of being the sons of a sea-god, the dynasty of the Jagellons in Poland were proud of their original descent from the Devil, no doubt through Killecroffs, and actually bore in their arms certain emblems of hell.

How can a real Killecroff be recognized, since he has been, improperly enough, counted in among the Kobolds?

From his first appearance in the world, the Killecroff excites the astonishment, and sometimes the

admiration of his reputed parents. He sucks so
heartily and with such an appetite that his nurse
has to be reinforced by two goats and a cow, like
the renowned Gargantua.

When he is weaned a new marvel appears : he
swallows his soup by the tureen, "as much as two
peasants and two threshers in the barn would
take," says a celebrated writer in speaking of this
subject.

He grows up and keeps everything in commo-
tion around him ; he provokes quarrels not only
among the servants, but even between his parents.
If some untoward event occurs he roars with laughter, on a day of rejoicing he sheds tears and moans
piteously. He takes a stick or a spit and rides on
it in his room, from morning till evening, climbing
on every chair and table, breaking everything that
comes in his way, injuring himself also quite as
readily, provoking cats, dogs, and even the parrot
on his perch, till they all mew and bark and scream.
Then he runs to the stable and sticks a pin into
the croup of a horse to see it kick, and then breaks
open the doors and locks by the aid of a huge
stick of wood ; next he rushes into the garden,
playing the part of a tempest there, destroying, up-
rooting, and breaking everything.

In the poultry yard he wrings the hens' necks
and walks over the young chickens; in the kitchen

he loves to take up the tops of pots and pans and to season the dishes according to his fancy with salt, pepper, dust, ashes, oil, vinegar, mustard, sand, or sawdust, and never leaves without having turned on the water everywhere.

If a visitor arrives, he takes possession of him and stands between his legs, and walks on his toes, pulls the buttons off his waistcoat, and draws the strings out of his shoes; he troubles and annoys him in every way, he pinches and scratches, he worries and tortures him. When his mother cautiously observes that he must not trouble the gentleman he obeys like a good child and leaves the gentleman alone, but not without having first broken his watch-chain, taken his cane, and hid his spectacles; the cane he drops accidentally into the well; as for the spectacles, he forgets where he has put them. When the poor visitor, quite overcome and exhausted, at last rises to go, he stumbles and falls down the stairs, thanks to a string which his playful young friend, the Killecroff, has stretched across the top step.

The Killecroffs are generally the delight of their parents; fortunately they do not live long.

The great man whom I have quoted before, told the Duke of Anhalt frankly, that if he were a sovereign like the duke, he would run the risk and become a murderer in such a case, by ordering every such son of the devil to be thrown into the Moldau!

This great man, who believed so firmly in Kille-croffs, who believed likewise in Butzemann, in Kobolds, in Nixen and Undines, who saw the Devil in every fly that came to drink his ink or to perch on his nose, was again Dr. Martin Luther.

The great Reformer, who was so valiant in combating the superstitions of the Papists, seems to have taken very little trouble to get rid of his own.

But among the many delusions, in which he apparently delighted, there was one, a really charming one, which arose from the Christian religion itself, and which, it seems to me, I cannot well pass over in silence when speaking of familiar spirits.

I mean Guardian Angels.

A most erudite and clever academician, Mr. Alfred Maury, tells us in his charming book on "Magic and Astrology," that according to Egyptian doctrines a special star foretold the arrival of every man in this world. In proof of this statement, he refers us to Horapollon, in his "Treatise on Hieroglyphics."

We infinitely prefer taking Mr. Maury's own evidence; and he adds: "This creed exists still in some remote districts among rural populations, and especially in Germany."

It may be that in certain portions of Germany every man may still have faith in his star; we are willing to believe it, since he says so; but almost everywhere the star has been superseded by a Guardian Angel, the White Angel, as they call him, a far more tempting personage, and infinitely more intimate and sympathetic. The White Angel is much more than the *Genius loci;* it is in fact the *Genius personalis.*

Without entering here upon a serious discussion, on the subject of Guardian Angels, whom the modern Church is disposed to ignore, we shall prefer

inserting here, as a complement to our chapter on
Familiar Spirits, a legend, which we were fortunate
enough to obtain directly from very truthful and
very beautiful lips : —

" A white figure appeared before the young girl
as she awoke.

" ' I am your Guardian Angel ! '

" ' Then you will grant me the wishes which I
shall mention ? '

" ' I shall carry them to God's throne. You may
count upon my assistance. What are your wishes ? '

" ' O White Angel, I am tired of continually turning the spindle, and my fingers are getting to be so
hard by constant work, that yesterday, at the dance,
my partner might have imagined he was holding a
wooden hand.'

" ' Your partner was that fine looking gentleman
from Hesse ? Did he not tell you that he adored
your blue eyes and fair hair, and that he would
make you a baroness, if you would go home with
him ? '

" ' White Angel, make me a baroness ! '

" The evening of that day a young peasant came
and asked Louisa's mother for her daughter's hand.
The mother said, Yes.

" ' White Angel, deliver me from this boor. I
want to be a baroness ! '

" But the mother, who was a widow, had energy

enough for two. The White Angel did not appear again; Louisa had to yield, and went on turning her spindle.

"One day her husband, who was a hard-working man, had over-exerted himself and was taken ill. Louisa had seen her gentleman again.

"'White Angel, he loves me still. He has sworn he would marry me if I were a widow.' . . . . She dared not say more. Her husband recovered his health completely. The White Angel still turned a deaf ear to her wishes. She lost all hope of ever becoming a baroness.

"Some years later Louisa was the mother of two beautiful children; she was fond of her husband, whose labor procured for her all that she needed, and when she thought of him and her two darlings, the spindle felt quite soft to her fingers.

"One evening, when she was only half asleep, lying by her husband's side, with one of her hands in his, and the youngest of her babies at her bosom, the white figure appeared once more and she heard a gentle voice whispering something into her ear. It was the voice of the White Angel.

"What did it say?

"It told her a fable.

"'A little fish was merrily swimming about in the water and looking seriously at a pretty blackcap which first circled around and around in the air and then alighted softly on a branch of a willow which grew close to the bank of the river.

"'"Oh," said the little fish, "how happy that bird is. It can rise up to the heavens and go high up to the sun to warm itself in its rays. Why cannot I do the same?"

"'The blackcap was looking at the fish at the same time, and said : —

"'"Oh! how happy that fish is! The element in which it lives furnishes it at the same time with food; it has nothing to do but to glide along. How I should like to sport in the fresh, transparent water!"

"'At that moment, a kite pounced upon the poor little fish, while a scamp of a schoolboy threw a stone at the bird; the blackcap fell into the water, the fresh, transparent water, and for a moment struggled in it before it died, while the little fish, carried aloft, could go up on high to the sun and warm itself in its rays. Their wishes had been granted.'

"'Louisa,' continued the gentle voice, 'our duty as Guardian Angels is far more frequently to thwart wishes than to satisfy them.'

"This was the moral of the fable.

"Louisa pressed her husband's hand warmly, kissed her last born, and said: 'Thank you, White Angel, thank you.'"

I am certainly delighted to think, that if the poor Germans have Killecroffs among their familiar spirits, they have at least also White Angels.

XIV.

XIV.

GIANTS AND DWARFS. — *Duel between Ephesim and Grommclund.* — *Court Dwarfs and Little Dwarfs.* — *Ymer's Sons.* — *The Invisible Reapers.* — STORY OF THE DWARF KREISS AND THE GIANT QUADRAGANT. — *How the Giants came to serve the Dwarfs.*

IF legendary tradition is only a distant vibration of the bell of history, where must we go and look for traces of the real existence of giants? Must we believe the Edda or Holy writ itself? Afterwards the great fossil skeletons of mammoths, mastodons, and other antediluvian animals only revived the memory of gigantic men. The Apocryphal Books tell us that in the days of Enoch, a number of angels, amounting to two hundred, had conceived a desire for the daughters of men and came down to Mount Hermon in order to be near them. Some of the principal ones are even mentioned by name; there were Urakabaramiel, Sanyaza, Tamiel, and Akibiel. Is it a wonder, then, that credulous people should have believed that devils also, who after all are but fallen angels, have acted in the same way towards the descendants of Eve. The Killecroffs, we have seen, were the offspring of a union between devils and earthborn women; in like manner giants were the offspring of marriages between women and angels. Women are evidently capable of setting heaven, earth, and hell on fire.

Germany, which was the last part of Europe to enter the great Catholic Church, and was to be the first to leave it again at the time of the Reformation, kept up the belief in giants longer than any other country. Perhaps this was one of the results of the right of free inquiry.

The giant Einheer lived in the days of Charlemagne and even served in his army. Several centuries later there were gigantic burgraves (Burggrafen), living all along the banks of the Rhine. They have a well known story there of a young and ingenious giant's daughter, who had been jealously guarded in her father's castle, and when she got out into the fields for the first time in her life, brought back in her apron a peasant with his plough and his two horses, whom she had picked up on the way. She showed them to her father as being all three little animals of very curious shape.

After a while, however, the giants became smaller and smaller, until there were only a few left in the highest mountains, in dark forests, and in the romances of chivalry. After that they disappeared altogether.

The report is, however, that a single couple, man and wife, are kept alive by magic art in an isolated part of the Hartz Mountains, to serve as a specimen of the lost race.

22

At first the giants had produced universal terror. The god Thor was blessed because he had driven them, armed as he was with his famous iron mace, all across the Hercynian forest. But as people became better acquainted with them, their fears subsided. They turned out to be far from cruel, to eat human flesh only in cases of dire necessity, and to act generally not only kindly, but even like simpletons — a misfortune common to most men, who are too fully developed in length or in breadth. This latter weakness is well supported by a popular German tale.

An old duke of Bavaria had at his court a dwarf, called Ephesim, and a giant, called Grommelund. The latter laughed at the dwarf, and Ephesim threatened to box his ears. Grommelund laughed only the more heartily and challenged Ephesim to carry out his threat. The dwarf accepted the challenge, and the duke, having been a witness of the whole scene, ordered at once that a field for single combat should be prepared.

Everybody expected to do as the giant did and laugh at the pigmy; as the poor little fellow was hardly two feet high and would have had to climb a long way before reaching the giant's ears. But it turned out very differently.

The dwarf began by walking all around the giant as if to take his measure. The good-natured giant,

standing up immovable, looks down upon him and
laughs till his sides
shake ; but while he is
holding his hands to
his sides, the dwarf un-
ties his shoestrings and
then worries him by
kicking and pinching
his calves.

Grommelund laughs
more loudly than ever,
thanks to the tickling,
takes a few strides,
steps on his loose
shoestrings, nearly stumbles, and at last, with a
thoughtful presence of mind, characteristic of his
race, he stoops down to tie the strings.

Ephesim has foreseen this, he avails himself of
the opportunity, and slaps the giant's cheek with
his little hand, so heartily that the sound reaches
the ears of the duke and the lords of his court,
who applaud Ephesim's skill enthusiastically.

The poor giant, humiliated and overcome, left
the town, it is said, and sought refuge in the mountains, where he died of shame.

The people were thus beginning to have a very
humble opinion of giants, when a rumor was spread
that they had entered the service of the dwarfs ;

not of court dwarfs, but of little dwarfs, who are so small that, by their size, the others appear as giants.

These little dwarfs appear in the popular tales of Germany, under different names, as *Wichtelmän-ner*, *Metallarii*, or *Homunculi*, and evidently, at

THE HUMILIATED GIANT. (p. 341.)

one time, were found in great numbers throughout all the mountainous parts of the North. In Bre-tagne they were also known as *Couribes*, *Parulpi-quets* or *Cornicouets*, but as they are ugly and evil disposed, I presume they are not of the same race with our good little dwarfs. These latter appear in the evening at the foot of large oak trees, or in old ruins, where they come by the thousand out

OUR GOOD LITTLE DWARFS.

of every crack and crevice and gambol and frolic, but vanish at the smallest noise.

As to their origin there are different opinions entertained. One theory alone is worthy of belief, because it is mentioned already in the Edda.

According to the Scandinavian Bible, when Odin had killed the giant Ymer, his decaying body produced an innumerable quantity of small worms. By a law of natural order which had already become operative with insects, each worm changed into a chrysalis, and out of each chrysalis came forth a little man, resembling, with a few trifling differences, the race of full sized men, whom Odin had created.

Like ourselves, they also are subject to all the infirmities of age, to disease and death; like ourselves, they are at times capable of reasoning with fairness. Skillful metallurgists, they are at work in the mines, where we have already met them; they are not without imagination, and even know what piety is.

What religion do they profess?

For a long time, we are told, the majority, having been converted to Christianity, were under its benign influence, in a far higher degree than we, for they did not carry on war among themselves, and all authors, legends, and ballads agree, that they were gentle and peaceful, loving each other,

kindly disposed towards others, laborious, and very
obliging. Hence they were universally known as
the *Peaceful People*, — das stille Volk.

" In ancient times," says Wyss, " men lived in
the valleys, and around their dwellings, in the cavi-
ties of the rocks, dwelt the little dwarf people,
keeping always on very good terms with them, and
helping them even at times in their work in the
fields. They took great delight in doing good in
this way; for generally they were very busy min-
ing in the mountains, and digging in the ground
to collect the tiny particles of gold and silver that
could be obtained."

Sometimes field laborers coming out to plant
or to weed, found their work already done, and
heard the dwarfs, hid behind the bushes, break out
into loud laughter, when they showed their amazement.

It happened one day, early in the morning, that
some peasants in passing a cornfield, saw that the
stalks were falling in long rows, as if by their own
will; they were most cunningly cut off below, and
now they were ranging themselves, also to all appearance by their own act, in long sheaves. The
peasants had no doubt that the good little dwarfs
were there, working away stealthily, but of the tiny
workmen not a trace could be seen.

The dwarfs possessed, in common with all these

mysterious races, the power of making themselves invisible. They had nothing to do, for that purpose, but merely to draw a little hood over their ears, which formed part of their costume.

Our countrymen, seeing that the wheat was not ripe enough to be cut, became exceedingly angry against these injudicious friends, and arming themselves with twigs, went to work striking right and left in the hope of hurting one or the other by chance. They really heard some faint cries of distress in the furrows, and soon the first rows of wheat which had been left standing were thrown into violent disorder, thus testifying to the flight of the little ones.

Several of the dwarfs became even visible, as the twigs suddenly tore the hoods from their heads. Thereupon the men became furious and tried to strike all the harder; but suddenly a violent storm broke forth and the hail came down in torrents, cutting the whole standing crop to pieces and sparing only the rows that had been reaped.

The rude countrymen now saw clearly that the Quiet People had foreseen the hailstorm and anticipated the harvest on that account. They repented their brutality, but the dwarfs, disgusted by their ingratitude, never again appeared in that region of country. Similar occurrences took place in other countries.

Now let us see, by what perseverance, by what skill, and especially by what audacious conceptions these tiny beings, not much more than a few inches high, succeeded in making themselves masters of the giants.

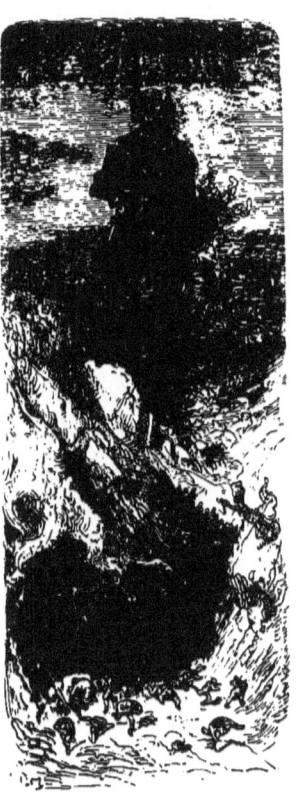

It is said, though without fixing a date, that in ancient times, one of the principal giants wanted a cane, perhaps to beat the dust out of his clothes, or perhaps merely to give himself a fashionable air in the presence of certain giant damsels, and thus pulled up a young oak sapling. Now it so happened that in the roots of that tree a whole nation of our myrmidons had been living for some time.

When the giant saw this host of little creatures, running about quite bewildered, pushing and jostling each other in their anxiety to regain their little mole-hill, he stood at first with his mouth

wide open, lost in amazement. Then, to amuse
himself in true lordly fashion, he crushed a few
dozen with his foot.

But he was not without curiosity, and hence he
tried in the next place to find out something about
their manners. The moment was not very well
chosen, it must be confessed. Men do not usually
choose a city that has just been taken by storm
and given up to pillage, for the purpose of studying the manners and customs of its citizens. But
we have seen before this, that giants are not re-
markably bright.

Our giant, whose name I have never been able
to ascertain and whom I will call for convenience
sake, *Quadragant* (" Quadragant was rather colossal," I once read in " Amadis of Gaul; " our giant
was really colossal, for he measured thirty feet in
height), our giant, I say, stretched himself out at
full length and fixed his eyes upon the hole out of
which he had pulled the oak tree. He heard a
low humming noise underground, but he could see
nothing.

He thought he would wait patiently, and in waiting he fell quietly asleep, turning over so as to lie
on his back, his usual position when he was sleeping.

After a few hours' sound and heavy sleep, such
as all giants are said to enjoy, he awoke. Finding

that the sun had in the mean time followed his example and gone to sleep, he remembered that it was supper time, and as he thought of the delights in store for him he uttered a long and deep sigh of satisfaction. But something that his long drawn breath had brought up, suddenly jumped out of his mouth.

This something was one of the dwarfs; and this dwarf, the boldest and most intelligent among them all, was called Kreiss.

But in order to make it clear how Kreiss happened to be almost in the giant's throat, which was of course only accidentally his home for a time, we must go back and see what had happened while Quadragant was asleep.

When the little pigmies found their tree uprooted and their people scattered in all directions, escaping through every crack and crevice in the soil, they had rushed into a long subterranean passage, excavated in days long gone by, by their forefathers. Here they had uttered their well known cries of distress, resembling the chirp of crickets, and thus they had finally reached the ruins of an old castle, inhabited by vast numbers of their people, and chosen as the place of meeting of the General Council of the dwarfs.

Kreiss happened to have arrived the night before, as one of a numerous deputation, and he at once suggested the propriety of burying the dead with all due honors, before anything else was done. After that, they might go to work stopping up all the holes and openings made by the tearing up of the sapling, and filling the excavation which it had produced, so that the rain might not come and inundate their long gallery, which was their only safe means of communication.

The two resolutions offered by Kreiss were carried by acclamation, and all, loaded with brush and with stakes, went immediately to work. There were some ten thousand of them.

They thought the giant had left, but they found him lying full length on the ground and snoring most fiercely. Their first impulse was to escape, but Kreiss held them back. He had conceived a bold plan ; he proposed to capture the giant. Were they not already provided with ropes and with stakes ? Was there not strength in numbers ? They immediately went to work, and in less than an hour the murderer, unable as he was to make the slightest motion, was bound to the soil which he had soaked with their blood.

"What do you say? . . . . Yes, sir, you are un-doubtedly right. This looks very much like the manner in which Gulliver was treated in the island of Lilliput. How can we help that? Besides, we must remember that there have been dwarfs in Germany from time immemorial. If Jonathan Swift undertook to transfer them to imaginary countries, whose business is that and who is liable to be charged with plagiarism, I ask you?"

We will not stop to discuss this trifling matter, which is of little importance. We have weightier matters than that in hand.

When the work was done and with the excite-ment of the efforts the first enthusiasm also had somewhat passed away, the question arose what was to be done with their capture. They looked at each other in great perplexity.

The dwarfs are kind hearted people, who have a great horror of blood. Besides, it would have been more difficult even, to dispose of the giant after death than to kill him. Still, if they did not kill Quadragant he would, as soon as he was awake, go to work and cry for help lustily; then the other giants would, no doubt, hasten to his assistance. The disgrace inflicted upon one of their brethren would in all probability render them furious, and they would proceed at once to uproot all the trees and to pursue the poor little people of dwarfs down into the very bowels of the earth.

While these and similar observations were passing in the crowd from one group to another, Kreiss remained silent and thoughtful, supporting his head in his hand and his hand on his elbow.

In the mean time the crowd passed from simple talk to grumbling and from grumbling to threats. There was nothing left but to undo what was done as promptly as possible, to abandon this ridiculous enterprise and to restore the giant to liberty in the same way in which he had been deprived of it — during his sleep. If he should awake before the operation was over, why, then they might try to appease his wrath by handing over to him the authors of this fatal project.

Ah! one can see at a glance, that these dwarfs, small as they were, were nevertheless men, and that it is better not to venture upon attacking giants!

They were utterly discouraged and demoralized. Calm in spite of all this excitement around him, Kreiss was still meditating, apparently quite unmindful of all the invectives that were hurled at him and the little hands that were threatening him. But when some of them actually began to loosen the ropes, he suddenly dropped his hands from his elbow and his brow, and turning sharply upon his aggressors, he said : —

" I acknowledge my mistake and I am ready to atone for it. Go, — my seven brothers and myself, we will alone set the giant free again. If he awakes, he shall have to do with us and with us only. Go ! "

The former conspirators were well content to accept the proposition, and without bestowing a thought upon their murdered brethren, they escaped as fast as they could. In the dim twilight of the last hour of the day one might have seen them running nimbly through the tall grass and under the cupolas of mushroom, arousing in their hurry the beetles and moths, or even mounting upon their backs in order to reach by their aid all the more quickly their safe retreat in the ruins of the old castle.

When all were gone save Kreiss and his seven

brothers, he said to them: "Now that we are alone, we alone shall reap the glory of the enterprise! So far from regretting what I have done,

FLIGHT OF THE CONSPIRATORS.

I mean on the contrary, to enlarge our project in a manner which shall redound to the eternal glory of our race."

The dwarfs are not only skillful metallurgists, but they are also most expert carpenters and builders.

Hence the good people of the Rheingau are

23

convinced that they have built all those ruins of
solid old castles, in which they are still living and
which they have so cunningly repaired and propped
up that they will last forever.

Now Quadragant was sleeping with his mouth
wide open, as all large people are apt to do. Kreiss
slipped boldly into this vast and spacious cavity,
armed with a long spear which was equally sharp

and pointed at both ends. He took care to rest
at first most cautiously only upon the projections
of the teeth, which formed, so to say, a double row
of parallel battlements. By such assistance he
passed from one end of the abyss to the other,
without troubling the slumbers of the giant by the

slightest awkwardness in his movements. For a case of emergency Kreiss held his spear firmly in his hands, ready to fasten it so between the two jaws as to prevent their closing upon him.

His brothers were in the meantime busily engaged in preparing posts, pins, and rafters, which they handed to him as he needed them. One of them even went with him to assist him.

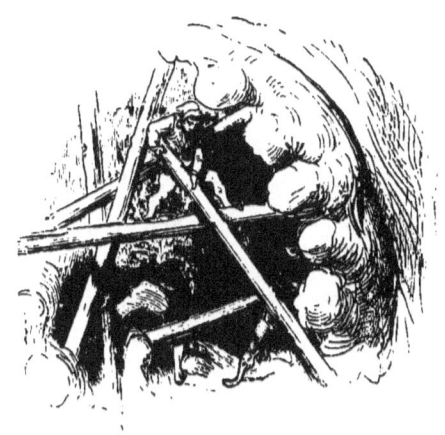

They fixed strong piles between the two rows of teeth, and strengthened the piles by beams, which secured them to each other. The work was by no means an easy one, for in the mouth of the giant it was as dark as night, and there reigned in it a heat equal to that of an oven. Moreover Quadragant had dined that day on a deer and several hares, and as he liked his game high, like every good judge of fine dinners, the perfumes of his breath increased the inconvenience caused by the heat and the darkness.

Kreiss's brother was all of a sudden taken ill, and had to leave to join the others outside. They, however, continued work on the scaffolding, and watched the giant carefully.

Quadragant was absolutely in the hands of the eight dwarf brothers.

They had passed up a lantern to Kreiss, which he hung upon one of the transverse beams, and he now continued his work alone resolutely, although he was every now and then compelled to stop his nose.

His work was at last completed, and he was just about to leave this damp, pestiferous abyss, when the giant awoke, and his first sigh carried off the brave pigmy, as a gust of wind would have carried off a dry leaf from a branch, and hurled him sense-less into space. He fell heavily upon the chest of the colossus.

As soon as he recovered from the shock, he looked around carefully, and saw, to his great satis-faction, that the bonds which held the giant were beyond doubt strong enough to hold him a pris-oner. Then he crept cautiously all along the neck as far as his ear, and by its aid climbed up the chin, after having crossed the cheek in its whole length. When he had found a convenient resting-place, he drew himself up to his full height, and raising his feeble voice as loud as he could, he said to the giant : —

"Murderer of our brethren, you are our prisoner, and you must die! Commend your soul to God."

The giant tried to see the tiny being who was speaking to him so boldly, and cast down his eyes. At first he could distinguish nothing but a feeble glimmering light at the extremity of his nose ; but the nose itself completely concealed the speaker.

Kreiss then advanced a few steps from the chin towards the mouth of the colossus, and the latter now perceived a kind of little man, dressed in a cloak of mouse skin, which he grandly wrapped around him, as Hercules did with the skin of the Nemean lion.

In his hand, however, he held not a club, but a lantern, in which a firefly did service as candle.

Thanks to this phosphorescent sheen, which seemed to surround Kreiss as with a halo, Quadragant could examine him at leisure, and he asked himself how such an embryo could have flown out of his mouth, and how he, Quadragant, could have become his prisoner ?

The contemptuous glance which he threw at the dwarf made Kreiss aware of what he was discussing in his mind.

"You think you are not captured yet," he said. "Very well, try to get up and walk, if you can!"

Quadragant did try, and found that he was firmly fastened to the ground by ropes and chains, by each single hair of his head, by every hair on his body. He tried to speak to the pigmy, and he could not, by any effort of his, move his jaws in the slightest way.

"As to the manner of your death," Kreiss went on, "if the wolves and the vultures do not hasten your end, hunger will do the work."

At this thought of dying of hunger, a mode of death which he had always looked upon as the most terrible of all, Quadragant's heart gave way, and he began to cry piteously. Two torrents of tears flowed down his cheeks, and after turning around the prominence of his lips, ran over from his chin.

Kreiss was compelled to leave his position, so as to avoid the double current.

Although quite firm in his resolution, he was naturally kind-hearted. These many tears of such unwonted size finally touched him, but his sympathy made him only the more determined to render his vengeance as useful as it was complete.

" Listen to me, giant. You can buy your life, if you choose." Quadragant's tears ceased to flow. Here was life offered to him, and with that life he

saw first of all a good supper in store for him, and if his mouth had not been held so tight by the scaffolding erected in it by Kreiss, his big face would have grinned from ear to ear.

" But," continued the dwarf, " you will have to devote your life and your liberty, if we restore both to you, to the service of our decimated people; do you hear? You must understand me clearly; you will not be our protector, but our servant; you will unhesitatingly perform every kind of work which may be required of you for our safety or our comfort. First of all you will replant that oak tree, under which the dwarfs of this district were living in peace, and you will water it every morning until it has taken root again. Now, close your eyes, if you mean to accept our conditions!"

Quadragant opened and shut his eyes quickly ten times in succession.

Kreiss made with his lamp a kind of telegraphic signal; his brothers, all seven dressed in garments of mouse skin or mole skin, and carrying each one a lantern with a firefly inside, climbed in an instant upon the face of the giant, which now looked quite brightly illuminated.

Three of them took their station on his forehead; two others by the side of each eye. The last two held each a long thorn in their hands, which they seemed to use as a dagger.

Kreiss, who had remained at his place, said again to the giant: —

"If, after you have been set free, you dare utter a sound to call for help, you lose both of your eyes instantly. Mind the warning!"

Armed with his double pointed spear, he then went once more into Quadragant's mouth, and loosened one of the transverse beams which formed the ceiling. The giant assisted him with his tongue in the work of demolition; then, after drawing a long sigh of relief, he closed his mouth and crushed between his formidable jaws all the timber, posts, and beams, as if they had been a bundle of matches, and swallowed the whole in anticipation of his supper.

After that he swore an oath which binds the giants as firmly as the invocation of the Styx pledged the gods of Greece.

" By the earth, which is my mother, by the mountains, which are her bones, by the woods and forests, which are her hair, by the brooks, the streams, and the rivers, which are the blood of her veins, I, the giant Quadragant, declare that I am the slave of the dwarfs."

At sunrise Quadragant was up again, carrying his new masters between his fingers, which he twisted together in the shape of a cradle. In less than five minutes he reached, in obedience to their orders, the old castle in ruins, where a solemn meeting was held, not only by the fugitives of the day before, but also by the principal representatives of all the dwarfs of that part of Germany.

When the sentinels announced the arrival of the giant, all thought their last hour had come and endeavored to escape, hoping to find a refuge in the lowest depths of the old building. Kreiss, however, had ordered the giant to put him down in front of the cellars of the castle, and now entered the great Meeting Hall, assuming like all great conquerors, an air of extreme modesty.

Then he informed them that the giant was their slave!

They at once threw themselves at his feet and expressed their desire to proclaim him Emperor of the Dwarfs.

Kreiss, however, having heard of a recent experiment of that kind, was far from believing such sudden enthusiasm to be either deep or permanent.

From that day the giant abandoned his old

KREISS ENTERING THE GREAT MEETING HALL.

name of Quadragant, and assumed that of *Putsku-chen*, which at that time meant Friend of the Dwarfs, but which, translated into modern German, represents our *omelette soufflée*.

At first all went well ; but at the end of three weeks Putskuchen looked sad and melancholy; Putskuchen only took half a dozen meals a day; Putskuchen was slowly fading away ; Puts-kuchen was in love, in love with a young giantess, who taunted him with having become the servant of these wretched pyg-mies and reproached him with his poverty. The unhappy crea-ture fell off more and more, the *omelette soufflée* fell down flat, and Putskuchen was a mere lath of thirty feet in length.

Kreiss had always felt a certain tenderness for him, and hence, after having asked the consent of all the other chieftains, he placed in the giant's hands a large heap of gold scales such as the dwarfs were in the habit of collecting in the neigh-boring mountains.

It was enough to buy three wives, instead of one.

The fact had no sooner become known than all

the happy giant fathers of the country desired him as a son-in-law, and when they saw how liberally his services had been rewarded by his new masters, they were all eager to become the serfs of the dwarfs.

Thus, thanks to Kreiss, the giants gradually came all, one by one, and entered the service of the dwarfs.

Certain skeptics have maintained that the whole story is symbolic.

According to their interpretation the giant fastened to the ground and muzzled by the dwarfs, is the people, the people always kept down and always held in subjection, in spite of its gigantic strength. The dwarfs, who lived under the oak, the sacred tree of all nations of Celtic origin, are the priests.

We say: Shame upon people, who would change a legend into an apologue and our friend Kreiss into a Druid!

When the dwarfs became reconciled again to men, they compelled the giants to execute for them great works of public utility, such as bridges and highroads, which were afterwards generally ascribed to the Romans.

The belief in little dwarfs continues to this day to exist in most of the Northern countries. They still live in myriads in the subterranean regions

and in the rocks in Westphalia, in Sweden, and in
Norway, and they are still hard at work amassing
vast treasures.

XV.

XV.

Teutonia ! — What became of the Ancient Gods. — Venus and the good Knight Tannhäuser. — JUPITER ON RABBIT ISLAND. — *A Modern God.*

HEAR ! hear ! New and greater marvels still ! But, unfortunately, we shall be under the sad necessity of returning to our giants once more, much as we have already spoken of them, from giant Ymer down to Quadragant, and there may be too much even of the best things in this world. But let the reader take courage ; this time my giants are not real giants ; or at least they are giants of a very peculiar species. But instead of losing time with limitations and explanations, let us begin our story.

It was in the days when the Scandinavian gods were still in the full enjoyment of their power.

One fine day the god Thor, curious to see certain distant lands of which they had told him most marvelous stories, set out on his travels, accompanied by Raska, Tialff, and Loki. Leaving Sweden and Norway behind, they arrived at the sea-shore and crossed over by swimming. A mere trifle, of course, for people of their kind. On the opposite shore they found a vast plain, and as night was approaching and they began to feel that rest would be acceptable, they looked out for a shelter. In this vast and deserted plain they see but one single building ; a huge, ill-shapen, and abandoned house, rather broad than high and of altogether exceptional appearance. It has neither doors nor windows, nor even a roof ; but the night fog may possibly conceal a part of the edifice. The travellers enter and find a square, low vestibule, and at the end of it five long passages; each of the travellers takes one of these passages, looking for a door or a bed in the dark. As they find neither bed nor chamber, they resign themselves and lie down on the floor, with their backs to the wall.

But even the walls seem to be elastic, and so does the floor ; .perhaps a layer of straw or of moss was spread over them and gave them the softness of felt, rather coarse, to be sure, but not unpleasant. The travellers felt that they could sleep there comfortably and warm. So they did.

At daybreak Thor rubbed his eyes, stretched his arms and proposed to take a turn in the country, to stretch his legs and to shake off the heaviness of sleep. Through the white mists which were still hanging on the tops of high hills he thought he saw a huge mass of disheveled hair, and then he discovered in the centre of that head two eyes. At first he thought this head and these eyes were simply a rock covered with shrubbery and two small pools of water shining in the rays of the rising sun. But soon the disheveled head began to move, bent down to the ground, and turned now to one side and now to another. In the meantime the mists had risen and Thor found that he was standing before a giant of such enormous size that those whom he was generally engaged in hunting down would not have reached to his knee.

The giant advanced toward him, always looking here and there, and still with his eyes fixed on the ground, as if he were looking for something he had lost.

Thor, who was easily incensed by the sight of a giant, went straight up to meet him and said in an arrogant tone: —

"What are you doing here? What is your name? Who are you?"

"My name is Skrymner," replied the other. "Did you not know? As for me, I have no need to ask you any such question; you are the god Thor, one of those under sized gods who live with Odin on the ash tree Ygdrasil. Have you seen my glove? I have lost my glove; yes! yesterday," he added in the most indifferent manner possible, and as if he were solely occupied with his search.

"I have found nothing of the kind," replied Thor, who was always in bad humor, and now regretted that he did not have his hammer at hand.

"And do you travel quite alone?" asked Skrymner.

" I have three companions."

" I do not see them."

" They are all three still asleep in that house there, in which we have spent the night."

And with his finger he pointed at the house, which they had used as an inn for the night.

Skrymner looked both surprised and delighted. " My glove!" he cried, " that is my glove! I have found it." He hastened to pick up this apparent house with its five long passages, and took it up, but not before he had shaken it, holding it close to the ground, and showing thus that he was not without a feeling of humanity.

Loki, Tialfi, and Raska tumbled out upon the grass, rather terrified by their sudden ascension and the sudden somerset which they had been forced to make. But as soon as they had recovered from their first surprise, and especially from the discovery that they had spent the night in a glove, they thought of continuing their journey.

The country was unknown to them, but Skrymner offered to act as guide and even to carry their baggage. So much obliging kindness and courtesy drove all aggressive thoughts out of Thor's mind, especially as he now had his hammer.

At the first stopping place, and just when they were getting ready for breakfast, the giant left them, although only after having pointed out to them the road they ought to take. Thor, however, found he was unable to open the knapsack in which they carried their provisions; all the strings and small chains by which it was fastened, were in knots. They had to proceed on their journey without having had any breakfast, a necessity which is most disagreeable to travellers, and even to gods.

As hour after hour passed and the plain remained deserted and sterile, their hunger became tormenting. They listened with all their might, hoping they might hear the roaring of a bear or the lowing of a cow, determined as they were to dine upon the one or the other; but the dull rumbling of a storm and the distant roll of thunder was all they heard.

Thor was furious at the idea that any one should venture to thunder without having obtained permission from him, the god of thunder, and rushed forward. Following the direction of the noise, he reached a rocky defile, overshadowed by a few oak trees, where he found Skrymner lying at full length between two hills and snoring furiously. This snoring it was which the travellers had taken for the roaring of a storm.

" No doubt," said Thor to himself, " the wretch is at work digesting the provisions of which he has robbed us. No doubt it was he who tied all those knots in the strings of our knapsack, in order to

conceal his theft; but he shall pay for it dear!
Besides, did he not speak of me as an undersized
god ? "

With these words he seized his hammer and
threw it at the head of the sleeping giant, who did
not stir, but only passed his hand over his brow
as if a dead leaf falling from a tree had tickled
him a little.

Thor went up closer and ˙struck him once more
on the back of his head, directly on the cerebellum,
which in giants is unusually developed.

This time the sleeper opened one eye, closed it
again, and after having scratched himself at the
place where he had been struck, he fell asleep
again.

Brutal by nature and doubly so when fasting, Thor
had become perfectly furious when he found himself thus mysteriously powerless. Fully determined
the next time to make an end, once for all, of his
adversary, he put on his invisible belt, which had
the gift of doubling his strength, seized his hammer with both hands and threw it with such amaz-
ing force at the giant, that it sank up to the
handle into one of his cheeks and Thor had no
small trouble in getting it to come back to him.

This time Skrymner was fully roused; he opened
both of his eyes, raised his hand to his cheek, and
exclaimed that it was impossible to sleep comforta·

bly in that place, as a fly had just stung him in the cheek.

Then, perceiving his assailant, who stood right before him, he asked him good-naturedly, how he happened to be there, and whether he had lost his way. In the meantime the other travellers are also coming up and Skrymner offers to show them the way to the great city of Utgard, where he promises they will find a good inn, a good table, a warm reception, and not only enough for their wants but all that their heart can desire.

Thor does not know what to think. Overcome and confounded, he follows the footsteps of his guide, without being able to form any idea except the one : to avenge himself in a signal manner for all his humiliations.

The city of Utgard is of incredible size, the city walls, the houses, the trees, the furniture, all are gigantic. Our travellers could easily pass between the legs of the little children they met in the streets, as we modern people pass under the triumphal arches of the ancients. You see, now we are no longer in Lilliput, we have reached the island of the giants with Gulliver. Gulliver might very well be the offspring of some Scandinavian legend.

The king received Thor and his friends, laughing heartily at their small size, and the seats they are offered are three times as high as they are.

After a host of adventures in which our men, that is to say, our gods, are continually victimized, Thor in his rage challenges the giants to single combat. The king accepts the challenge and offers to back his nurse, a toothless old woman, against the god. Thor consents, eager as he is to vent his wrath on somebody, and determines to pitch His Majesty's nurse out of the window. But by all his efforts he hardly succeeds in lifting her slightly off the ground, and he himself, exhausted by the struggle, sinks on his knees.

On the next day our travellers came to the conclusion that they had travelled far enough. Skrymner again showed the way, with his usual courtesy, and when they were well out of the town he took the god Thor aside and said to him : " So far you have only known my name and nothing of myself, now you ought to know that I am Skrymner, the wizard. You ought, therefore, not to mind anything that has happened to you during these last days. You thought you were striking me three times with your hammer, but in reality you were striking the impenetrable rocks, on which I was apparently sleeping. As to the nurse, you have given proof there of such strength as I should not even have expected from the great Thor, when you lifted her from the ground ; for the toothless old woman is none other but Death, yes Death,

whom I had compelled to come and take part in
our games. The rest was all enchantment, mere
delusions! I wanted to see if the power of the
art of Magic was equal to that of the gods. Farewell, Asa-Thor, and a pleasant journey to you."

More enraged than ever, Asa-Thor was about to
throw himself upon him ; but the pretended giant
had fled in the shape of a bird. Then Thor turned
back towards the city of Utgard, determined to
destroy it utterly, but before his eyes it dissolved
into a column of smoke.

Well, I promised you some of Mother Goose's
stories — have I kept word ? And do not imagine
that this story of Thor and the giants' city is of
doubtful origin — you will find it in chapters 23, 24,
25, and 26 of the sacred book called Edda.

Of magicians and wizards I could say much, but
the road is long and I am in haste to reach the
end. And who does not know the story of the
prowess of Merlin and of the Maugis ?

In all the ancient traditions of the North there
are found innumerable tales of wizards, witchcraft,
and ghosts. Now rocks are changed into palaces,
and now brutes into men and men into brutes ;
and the same fantastic but always epic element
prevails largely in all the old romances of chivalry
as well as in the great poems of Ariosto and
Tasso.

In almost all countries we find that epic poetry is closely allied to religious sentiments and through these to the marvelous ; for it has always found a first home in temples and a first use for temples. Thus it was in India with the Mahabarata, and in Greece with the myths of Hercules and of Orpheus. It could not be otherwise with the Gallic or German bards, nor with the Scandinavian skalds, all of whose grand poems are most unfortunately unknown at present.

But a feature more peculiarly German than the wizards, are the bewitched, often called the *Sleepers.* In these Germany incorporates, as it were, the loftiest of her patriotic aspirations, the saddest of her disappointments, the most persistent of her hopes. They represent not only her old faith, that could never be completely eradicated, but also her old favorites, a Hermann and a Siegfried, the hero of the Nibelungen, a Theodoric and a Charlemagne, a Witikind and a Frederick Barbarossa, a William Tell and a Charles V. Her heroes, her beloved, her glory — she has not allowed them to fall into oblivion and be severed from the present ; she will not admit that they are dead, they are but asleep. Witikind under the Siegberg in Westphalia, Charlemagne in the lowest rooms of his old castle at Nuremberg. There — and not, as might have been imagined, in Aix-la-Chapelle — the mighty old

Emperor rests majestically, surrounded by his brave champions, ready to awake again whenever God shall be pleased to tell him that the moment has come.

As for Frederick Barbarossa, he sleeps in the Kyffhäuser, one of the porphyry and granite mountains of the Taunus, and so do others; there is no denying the fact, for they have been seen!

A few years after his disappearance from this world, Frederick showed himself upon the summit of one of these mountains, whenever the sound of a musical instrument was heard in the valley. Knowing his love of music, the Philharmonic Societies of Erfurth and of other towns to this day, are fond of serenading the old warrior.

It is said that one evening, when the clock at Tilleda struck midnight, certain musicians who had ascended the Kyffhäuser, suddenly saw the mountain open and a number of women adorned with jewels and carrying torches, came out of the opening. They beckoned to them, the men followed, continuing to play on their instruments and thus they came where the Emperor was. The latter ordered a good supper to be served, and when they were ready to leave again, the fair ladies of the court escorted them back, with their torches in their hands, and at the last moment gave to each of them a poplar branch. The poor musicians had hoped for better things from the Emperor's gene-rosity, and when they reached the foot of the mountain, they threw their branches into the road, very indignant at having been so badly treated. Only one among the number kept his branch, and when he reached home, carefully stuck it by the side of the consecrated bunch of box which hung over the head of his bed. Immediately, O marvel! each leaf of the poplar branch changed into a gold ducat. When the others heard of this, they has-tened to look for their branches, but they never found them again.

On another occasion a shepherd — others say a miner — met on the Kyffhäuser a monk with a white beard, who unceremoniously and just as if he had asked him to come and see his next door neighbor, told him to come with him and see the Emperor Barbarossa, who wanted to speak to him. At first the poor shepherd was dumb-founded; then he began to tremble in all his limbs. The monk, however, reassured him and led him into a narrow, dark valley, and then, striking the ground three times with his rod, he said : "Open! open! open!"

Thereupon a great noise arose beneath the feet of the monk and the shepherd; the earth seemed to quake and then a large opening became visible. They found they were in a long gallery, lighted up by a single lamp and closed at the other end by folding doors of brass. The monk, who no doubt was a magician, knocked three times at the door with his rod, saying again : "Open! open! open!" and the brass doors turned upon their hinges, producing the same noise which they had heard before underground.

They were now in a grotto, whose ceiling and walls, blackened by the smoke of an immense number of torches, seemed to be hung with black as a sign of mourning. It might have been taken for a mortuary chapel, only there was no coffin or catafalque visible. The shepherd had, in the mean time, begun to tremble once more, but the monk repeated his summons before a silver door, which thereupon opened in the same manner as the brass door.

In a magnificent room lighted but dimly and in such a manner that it was impossible to tell where the light came from, they saw the Emperor Frederick, seated upon a golden throne, with a golden crown on his head ; as they entered he gently inclined his head, contracting his bushy eyebrows. His long red beard had grown through the table before him and fell down to the ground.

Turning, not without visible effort, towards the shepherd, he spoke to him for some time on different subjects and recommended to him to repeat what he heard to his friends at home. His voice was feeble, but it grew strong and sonorous as soon as he alluded to the glory of Germany. Then he said : —

"Are the ravens still flying over the mountains ? "

" Yes! " replied the shepherd.

"Are the dead trees still hanging over the abysses of the Kyffhäuser as in former days ? "

" Who could uproot them, unless it be a great storm ? "

" Has no one spoken to you of the reappearance of the old woman ? "

" No ! "

" Well then, I must sleep another hundred years ! "

He made a sign to the shepherd that he could go, and then fell asleep, murmuring the name of a woman which died on his lips.

For among these great *Sleepers* of Germany there is also a woman, but a woman rather of symbolic than real existence. What is the difference ? Tradition gives the following account of her : —

When Witikind was beaten by Charlemagne at Engter, a poor old woman, unable to follow him in his flight, uttered lamentable cries and thus added to the panic among the defeated army. When the

25

soldiers obeyed Witikind's orders and stopped for a moment in the heat of their flight, they threw a mass of sand and rock upon the old woman. They did not expect that she would die when thus buried alive; their commander had told them: " She will come back ! "

This old woman, who is to come back, is Teutonia, and it was her name that Frederick Barbarossa was murmuring to himself as he fell asleep for another century.

When the old woman shall have succeeded in extricating herself from this mass of sand and rock which weighs her down, then and then only the great day will come. The heroes who now are held captive in their mountains and subterranean grottoes, will shake off the torpor of their long sleep; they will reappear among their people, the dead trees will bear new foliage to proclaim their return by a miracle, and the cry of : Teutonia ! Teutonia ! will resound in a thousand valleys, and the birds even will repeat the name !

They say that when this long wished for day does come, Germany will be freed of all her difficulties, and will boast of having but one creed, one law, and one heart; she will be glorious and free, one and indivisible !

We must wait for the birds to tell us so, before we believe it.

At that time Teutonia and her emperors were alike asleep. They mention a peasant woman from Mayence, who on her way home became so exhausted and unable to bear the heat of the sun, that she had to seek shelter in an isolated house, standing by the wayside in the midst of a plantation of young trees. It was a dwelling of a skillful magician. She asked him for leave to rest there a few moments. As he was in the midst of some of his most abstruse calculations, he only replied by nodding his head, and glanced with his eye at a bench in the most distant part of the room. She went and sat down, but only on the edge, hardly knowing if she was allowed to do so or not; every moment she got up to ask her host if she disturbed him, and if she had not better leave him, tired and exhausted as she was. She told him that she would much rather endure the heat and the fatigue, than be a burden to him, she begged him not to mind her and to go on just as if she were not there, and a host of similar phrases.

Annoyed by her incessant, idle talk, the magician suddenly turned round and fixedly looked her full in the face. Immediately she fell asleep. (There was no doubt some knowledge of magnetism already in the world at that time, but as yet only of magic magnetism). When the good woman awoke, she was alone; her host had left her. To her great regret she was compelled to leave without being able to thank him for his hospitality in her usual profuse manner, and to beg him to excuse her falling asleep, when he did her the honor of keeping her company.

As she left the house, she was not a little surprised to see around the house, not a copse of young trees, but a number of tall pine trees and noble oaks, but she thought it possible she might have left by another door than that by which she had entered.

When she at last reached her village, new surprises were in store for her. Of all the good people whom she met on her way or whom she saw standing in the doors of their houses, she could not recognize a single one; she had to look a long time before she found her own house, and when she reached it at last, it was inhabited by strange people, who in spite of her protestations, pushed her out and treated her as mad.

Then followed a lawsuit, the result of which was to prove, that instead of sleeping an hour or so on that bench, as she believed, she had been asleep there a hundred years. Thus the young saplings had had time to grow up into large trees and her house to change masters. The strangers who were now living in it and who had turned her out so unceremoniously, were nothing less than her great grandchildren.

I hope, however, the matter was settled amicably.

The Germans have, with that perseverance which characterizes the nation, preserved all that could be preserved of their ancient gods as well as of their former heroes; they do not like to lose anything, only they did not embalm their favorites, but used enchantment. Let us, however, notice at once for the honor of the gods, that they were never condemned to sleep indefinitely. Not one of them is found among the great Sleepers, such as Charlemagne, Witikind, Frederick I., William Tell, or the peasant woman, from the neighborhood of Mayence. It is true, they were exiled to certain remote districts, which they were not allowed to leave, but they could at least move about and continue their former mode of life there, after a fashion.

It is not so very long since certain charcoal burners protested that they had seen Asa-Thor, for want of giants to combat, hurl his hammer against the tallest trees, which he broke and uprooted.

They had also seen the enchanted hunt of Diana, whose deep-mouthed dogs bark at night and disturb the slumbers of honest people in

Bohemian villages. Who has not heard of the intrigues of old Venus, not with her former, classic
lover, the god Mars, but with the good knight
Tannhäuser?   If   we   are   to   believe   Heinrich

Heine, even Jupiter
has been recently
discovered again in
one of the Norwe-
gian islands.

It would be the
height of impru-
dence, of course, to
undertake an ac-
count of the discov-
ery, after such a
master. I shall, therefore, be content to present a
mere summary of this remarkable tradition.

There is an island in the Northern seas, which
is bordered by icebergs and arid mountains: the
valleys are dim and dark with heavy mists, the
mountain tops are covered with snow for nine
months of the year.

Here, one dismal morning, some travellers
landed, driven by a tempest much more than by
their own free will. They were mostly savants,
members of great academies from Stockholm and
St. Petersburg, who had undertaken a voyage of
discovery to the polar regions. The arid, almost

bare soil did not promise a pleasant resting place, but the mountain slopes towards the south produced fine grass and dwarf gooseberry bushes, and the immense number of holes in the ground, together with distinct traces of débris left at the openings, proved that the island was at all events inhabited by countless numbers of rabbits. Of other animal life, however, no trace could be found.

Rabbits seemed to be the only inhabitants of the island, and that was tempting enough for poor sailors who had for some time been put on salt rations.

Our savants prepared, therefore, a large number of traps and snares, when suddenly a fierce tempest of snow and hail broke out, and compelled them instantly to seek refuge in a spacious cave which opened in that direction.

They were not a little surprised to find here an old man, bald, hollow cheeked, and pale, whose body was emaciated and decrepit and who was hardly clothed in spite of the rigor of the climate. But beneath all these signs of extreme old age, and great destitution, the stranger displayed an air of authority, and on his serene and lofty brow such supernatural majesty, that the travellers were filled with respect and reverence, and well-nigh trembled at his appearance.

An eagle of the largest variety, but so reduced that he looked the mere skeleton of a bird, and with faded and disheveled plumage, sat in a corner, the picture of misery, with his dull eyes and his drooping wings. He was the old man's sole companion.

The two hermits, having no other means of subsistence, lived by hunting, and the old man found in addition, means to carry on a modest traffic in the furs of the only game that the island contained; he laid up large supplies of the small peltry and exchanged it for luxuries. . . . .

But my pen refuses to go on. I cannot reconcile it to my principles as an author nor to my conscience as an honest student of genuine myths, to repeat here a story, which is altogether apocryphal, and which belongs much less to tradition than to mystification.

Now, this old man was Jupiter, and as I think it over, I come to the conclusion that Mr. Heine, who laughs at the most serious things, has skillfully concealed his irony under the cloak of an interesting story, for the mere purpose of telling us that the Chief of the Gods, dread Jupiter, has become — a dealer in rabbit skins!

I cannot follow his example.

Without wandering from my subject, for I am still speaking of false gods, I will substitute for this necessarily much curtailed account, another story which I can warrant as authentic.

"In Persia," we are told by Count Gobineau, in a recently published book of great merit, "the *Soufys*, that is to say the savants and philosophers, reject all dogmatic religion and believe in the reunion of the soul with God in trances only. When this union is complete, the soul is transformed and becomes itself a participant in the nature of the uncreated essence, and Man is God." Human folly is always a disease produced by human pride.

France, also, has produced a few gods of that kind; I do not mean to mention them, however, as belonging to the myths of the Rhine, which have special reference to Germany only. But among the Germans, also, there is a school of philosophers who without going as far as the Persians go, are utterly incredulous, and disregarding trances and immortal souls alike, have finally denied the existence of God altogether and made themselves gods. This shows how anxious savants as well as ignorant men are, in that beautiful country, to people the earth with deities of every kind!

It is the history of one of these earth-born gods which I propose to give here, before I close this long chapter. Alas! he is dead now, and that is a great pity; but he did live once; on that essential point there is no lack of evidence. I could even, like the Thuringian peasants when speaking of Frederick Barbarossa, say: " I have seen him! "

In the year 1800 there was born in Dusseldorf, in Prussia, a child in a Jewish family recently converted to Christianity. This child might well have been looked upon as of supernatural origin, so entirely different was it, from its earliest days, from all that had ever been seen before. Martin Luther no doubt, if the child had been one of his own, would have pronounced him to be a Killecroff.

He was not only noisy and troublesome, but he was also a pedant; he snubbed professors and listened to the advice of very young children. When his parents scolded him, he only laughed at them; when a grave event disturbed a neighbor's household, he laughed; when the French took his native city, he laughed; in fine he was always laughing.

However, as he grew up, he gorged himself with logic, with mathematics, with Greek and Latin and Hebrew and all kinds of good things besides. He became even a philosopher before he was of age, but his philosophy consisted mainly in a sarcastic laugh. When they spoke to him of the position he might occupy in Dusseldorf, and of the wealth he might acquire, his only answer was a grimace.

A rabbi spread out before him heaps of gold,

promising to give him that and more, if he would be his slave only for a few years; he refused to listen to him. As he was a vain man, the demon of Fame endeavored to tempt him, but he laughed in his face.

At last the devil, a real devil, I am sure (his name was George William Frederick Schlegel) whispered into his ear: " Would you like to be a god?"

This time our young philosopher did not laugh. He became a god, and, from official jealousy, proceeded to deny the great God in Heaven until he lost all human sentiments. He lived alone, friendless, childless, without a family and giving up even his mother country, finding that everything had to be done over again in this world, which he had not created.

After leaving Germany he came to France, and here in France he laughed louder and bitterer than ever. In France they did not believe in his divinity; they did not worship him, but they loved him as if he had been a simple mortal; in France he made friends and he became like other men once more. Finally, as he was after all bad only in his wit, he became voluntarily a convert as he saw the evil fruit of his teachings. He took a wife to himself with the sanction of the Church, and he died a believer.

This ex-god was called Heinrich Heine, that Heinrich Heine, who laughed so bitterly at his ex-colleague, Jupiter, and spoke of him as a dealer in rabbit skins.

XVI.

XVI.

WOMEN AS MISSIONARIES, WOMEN AS PROPHETS, STRONG WOMEN
AND SERPENT WOMEN. — *Children's Myths.* — *Godmothers.* —
Fairies. — *The Magic Wand and the Broomstick.* — THE LADY
OF KYNAST. — *The World of the Dead, the World of Ghosts,
and the World of Shadows.* — *Myths of Animals.*

WELL? Have you seen enough of the gods and
demigods of Germany, of the Nixen and goblins,

the Kobolds, the giants, and the dwarfs? Have I shown you enough of this vast storehouse of human folly? I must confess, it makes me melancholy to speak of all this, and I feel an urgent desire to "shut up shop."

The conscientious collector of myths, who has more material than he can manage, and sees new myths continually rising before him, is not unlike those learned physicians who spend their lives among crowds of insane people. A fever of imitation seizes them and soon they begin to wander like their patients.

Perhaps I have reached that point myself without becoming aware of it. The reader must judge for himself.

My mind, filled with myths, symbols, and eccentricities, is ready to ask for mercy, and still I feel it, there are some things yet to be done. For instance, I recollect having promised to give a completion of the history of the Druidesses, that is to say, of women, those myth-like beings by eminence! That kind of instinctive sense, that delicacy of almost intuitive perceptions which distinguished them from the other sex in its material coarseness, could not fail to give them easily the advantage over men. In Celtic lands as in Scandinavia they were the models of all virtues, the oracles of the house. They were occasionally beaten, it is

true, but they were also grandly honored, and in Germany especially people burnt incense before them, long before they smoked tobacco in their presence.

At the time when Christianity came, the women played a prominent and truly glorious part there; all the historians bear witness. Between the fourth and the sixth century Fritigill, Queen of the Marcomanni, Clotilda, Queen of France, and Bertha, Queen of England, had compelled their husbands to bow down before the Cross, and not by witchcraft, as the pagans wickedly maintained, but simply by persuasion. Other women, who belonged to noble families or to the common people at large, a Krimhild, a Thekla, and a Liobat, assisted the missionaries in their dangerous enterprise and actually helped them in cutting down the sacred oak trees.

What had become, during these long continued persecutions, of you, fair Gann, noble Aurinia, majestic Velleda, and of your sisters, the other Druidesses?

They were wandering about in dark forests, proscribed and weeping over their departed glory; they concealed themselves in remote places where the agents of the civil power but rarely appeared. Sometimes, of an evening, they would venture forth, approach a belated traveller on a cross-road, and hold with him mysterious converse. Sometimes, also, the inhabitants of a village, or even of a larger place, would go secretly to their well chosen hiding places to consult them on the good or evil chances of their prospects in life, or on an epidemic that was attacking their cattle. Some people, and among them not unfrequently recent converts, who were still strongly imbued with their former creed, would ask them to name their new-born infants and thus to bring them good luck. Hence they were at first known as *Godmothers*, and at a later time as *Fairies*.

It was naturally supposed that like the ancient fairies of the East, these women also derived their power from the stars, for why else should they have been met so constantly on the mountain slopes, when the moon was shining brightly, or slipping suddenly from behind a rock or a tree, where will-o'-the-wisps and fireflies alone were in the habit of being about?

Among these fairies many were kind and naturally benevolent; others, no doubt embittered by their fate, appeared irascible and ill disposed. Woe to the men, or even the cattle upon whom they cast an evil eye!

This evil influence could be averted only by the assistance of another fairy, a good one in this case, who relieved you more or less promptly by means of a talisman, a constellated stone, or certain words possessed of magic power.

Now, if we add to these godmothers, to these godchildren, to good and bad fairies, the terrible Ogres, whose very name filled the people of those days with terror, you will know all the mysterious personages which appear in the myths of children and which we have all known in our early days.

If we were to examine these legends and traditions more carefully, we should no doubt easily find "Bluebeard" again among the old burggraves of the Rhine, as "Puss in Boots" has already been discovered there. "The Sleeping Beauty" might very well be the peasant woman who had slept a century under the influence of magic magnetism, and why should not our little dwarf Kreiss and his brothers have furnished the first idea of little Tom Thumb, with Quadragant to play the part of the ogre? In "Cinderella" we might with the same readiness recognize one of the three Undine sisters, who forgot amid the delights of the evening assembly, that their furlough was out at ten o'clock? The same would apply, no doubt, to many others who lived under the influence of wicked Nichus or evil disposed fairies.

Poor Druidesses! If you had at least survived as fairies! If they had met you only in the air travelling simply by the aid of your magic wand!

But in proportion as Christianity increased, your power necessarily decreased. The day came at last, when they dared transform you into fortune tellers,

and finally into accursed witches! Then your en-chantress' wand became that atrocious broomstick upon which you travelled through the air on your way to the witches' Sabbath! Oh misery! Oh wretchedness ! What a fatal overthrow of all earthly glory and grandeur !

When the women thus saw their power of ruling men by prophetic inspiration slip away from them, they one fine day determined to change their tactics, their ways and manners, and, I am sorry to have to say it, almost their sex ! They assumed the noisy and truculent manners of their brothers and husbands and affected violent exercises, riding on horseback, wrestling, and even fighting in battles. This was the age of bullying women, of *Strong Women* in fact.

When they were young ladies they would admit no lover who could not prove his affections by the most perilous adventures and impossible enterprises. Such was the case with the famous Lady of Kynast.

She owned a large domain and on this domain a ruined old tower which stood on the summit of a steep, high rock, surrounded on all sides by a deep abyss.

Rich, young, and beautiful, eagerly sought for by a number of admirers, she did not think, in her desire to keep them from becoming too pressing, of undertaking an endless piece of embroidery like Penelope. She did not embroider ; in fact, she looked with contempt, and almost with disgust, upon every kind of work that was done by women.

She told her lovers that she was betrothed to Kynast — this was the name of the old tower — and
that any one who thought of winning her good
will, would first have to compete with her betrothed. To do this, nothing was required but to
climb up the rock and the tower, and after having
reached the battlements, to make a complete round,
not on foot, however, and assisted by the hands
and knees, but on horseback, without other assistance than the bridle.

The flock of lovers took flight instantly; only
two remained. They were two brothers, bereft of
reason by the strength of their passion.

After having cast lots, the first one attempted
the task and at first he was successful. But that
was all. He had no sooner reached the crenelated
top of the old tower, unaccompanied by his less
active courser, than he was seized with vertigo and
fell instantly into the abyss.

The second brother, in his turn, climbed up to
the top and actually succeeded in riding some
length along the battlements; but soon his horse,
feeling the stones slipping from under its hoofs,
and the whole tower rocking under the weight, refused to go on. To return was as impossible as
to proceed. The knight, determined to carry
through the undertaking in which he was engaged,
encouraged his horse with his voice and with his

spurs, but the poor animal remained immovable, apparently wedged in between the large stones of the tower. At last, knight and horse disappeared together; the abyss swallowed up their bleeding, mangled remains.

The Lady of Kynast could not disguise her delight and her pride as she received the congratulations of her noble neighbors; all the great ladies thought of having a Kynast, or a similar trap, in which they might catch and try their lovers.

No other claimants, however, appeared to woo this fair lady, who was so well protected by her betrothed. The poor damsel felt rather aggrieved by this neglect. She was by no means satisfied with having sacrificed only two young men to her pride; she was gradually becoming soured and ill-tempered, when at last a third lover presented himself and asked leave to attempt the trial.

She did not know who it was, and this surprised her; for how could he have fallen in love with her? He might possibly have seen her on her balcony, or at some royal feast; perhaps he was only allured by her great reputation. However, there was nothing to lose by accepting his offer. At best, he was only one more victim to be added to the list; that was all. At that time women were ferocious.

For some days a thick, heavy fog had shrouded

the castle and the old tower from top to bottom, so as to make the ascent utterly impossible.

The simple laws of hospitality, required, therefore, that the lady should offer her castle to the newly arrived knight.

The latter was handsome and of fine figure; his features beamed with bravery and intelligence; his white, delicate hands, exquisitely shaped, proved sufficiently that he was of noble descent; and his large retinue bespoke his high rank and large fortune. During three days he spent almost all his time with the young lady, but as yet he had not dared say a word of his love. She, however, felt herself gradually conquered by a feeling which had, until now, been unknown to her heart.

When the dense veil of mist was at length torn aside, and the Kynast shone forth in its full splendor, she was on the point of telling the knight that she would not insist on the trial in his case; but what would her good friends, the noble ladies of the neighborhood, have said?

When the moment came, the Lady of Kynast felt her heart fail her. She shut herself in, she wept, she cried, and although little given to prayers generally, she besought God to do a miracle in behalf of her knight. She could, however, hope very little from such a miracle, for in the meantime, loud clamors had been heard below, and as she

"SHE HAD REJOINED HER VICTIMS." (p. 415.)

surely thought the spectators were bewailing the death of her last lover, she fainted away.

Cries of joy and of triumph roused her again; the knight had successfully accomplished the task. Quite overcome, she rushes to meet him, and in her intense excitement and the depth of her passion, she forgets that all eyes are upon her, and breathlessly cries out: " My hand is yours."

But he draws himself up to his full height, and haughtily and harshly he replies with a withering smile : —

" Have I ever asked you for your hand? I only came to avenge my two brothers, whom you have killed, and I have done it, for I do not love you, and you love me! Very well! Now you can die of your love, or of your shame, as you like it! Farewell, I am going back to Margaret, my darling, my wife ! "

The same evening the wretched lady had herself hoisted up to the top of the tower, from whence she wished, as she said, to watch the setting sun. But before the sun had sunk below the horizon, she had rejoined her victims at the foot of the ruined old tower.

Thus the Kynast obtained possession of his betrothed.

The story might furnish an admirable plot for a grand opera. But, upon reflection, I think it would suit a circus better, for there are in it three first-class parts for horses.

The Lady of Kynast was a strong minded woman, rather than a really strong woman ; but there were others, who really distinguished themselves by extraordinary physical strength. It would seem that the habit of taking violent exercise had finally developed their muscles and sinews to such a degree, that few men could be found strong enough to overcome them in a wrestling match, or in armed combat.

Such was the noble Brunehilt, queen of Isenstein, in Norway.

Soothsayers, Godmothers, Fairies, Strong Women, and *Serpent Women* are not the only women of this class which we ought to mention here perhaps. We might also speak of the *Swan Women,* who floated on the water in the dim morning mist, clothed in a cloak of eider down ; and the *Forest Woman,* who was honored every year by the burning of a spindle full of hemp, to keep her from doing any harm ; and the *Water Sneezers,* to whom you had to say three times " God bless you ! " in order to save their souls from purgatory ; and the little *Moss Gatherers,* who could not escape from their enemies, the Forest Woman and the Wild Huntsman, unless a benevolent charcoal burner would mark some trees with three crosses, behind which they could conceal themselves. But we must make haste to conclude.

However, as the great *Wild Huntsman* has accidentally been mentioned, we do not think it would be fair to leave him out and pass him over in silence.

He is the Lord Hackelberg. Most imprudently he had begged God to allow him to exchange his

place in heaven for the right to hunt upon earth for all time to come. To punish him, God granted

27

his prayer, and ever since he has been hunting, with horns blowing and dogs barking, without respite or repose. He hunts continually, day and night, to-day as yesterday; he must hunt to-morrow as he does to-day, and yet he must hunt the same deer, which forever escapes from him, and ever will escape.

Which of the two is most to be pitied, the everlasting huntsman, or the everlasting game ?

How many others could claim a right to be mentioned here as well as he?

These are the people who are *condemned to remain standing forever*, and those who are *condemned to dance forever*, another variety of bewitched people.

You do not think my material is all used up? By no means! In the first place, I might have told you all about mythological animals ; of Thor's *buck-goat*, which enjoyed the same privilege as the boar of the Walhalla, of daily satisfying the powerful appetite of its master and his guests, and yet being replaced in all its bodily fullness, provided only care had been taken to put all the bones aside.

I might have gone back to give a fuller account of that famous Iormungandur, the great sea serpent, which still exists in our days — who dares doubt it ? The crew of an English vessel, passen-

gers, officers, and sailors, have unanimously testified
in a legally drawn up deposition that they have
met it quite recently in the Northern seas. What
more evidence do you want?

And the *Kraken*, that most marvelous of all
cetaceans, which could easily be mistaken for a
habitable island, and on which imprudent naviga-
tors once really landed, erecting their tents and
saying mass, without its ever stirring, until they
hoisted anchors, when the animal for the first time
gave signs of life?

And the *Griffins*, those perfect symbols of avarice, who are all the time busily engaged in drag-
ging forth from underground vast heaps of gold
and precious stones, merely in order to guard and
defend them ever afterwards, at the peril of their
lives, although the gold and the jewels are of no
use to any one? And Sleipner, Odin's *eight-legged
horse*, and the dog *Garm*, etc?

Passing on to another variety of zoölogical marvels, I might have mentioned the *Salmon*, whose
scaly skin wicked Loki assumed as a disguise in
order to escape from the wrath of the gods after
Balder's death. And that marvelous *Sturgeon* in
the Rhine, which the French legends have put to
good profit. Let us pause a moment in contemplation of this wonderful fish.

A young, noble lady determined, in order to save

her honor, to destroy her beauty, the grandest, most heroic, and most calamitous sacrifice that can possibly be made. Hence, when the moment for action arrived, her courage failed her. But if she could not bear the idea of becoming ugly, she could at least mutilate herself. So she puts her dagger upon the ledge of a window which over-looked the Rhine, seizes a hatchet, and with a single blow cuts off her hand, which falls into the river, and then with the bleeding stump terrifies her infamous persecutor. Here the sturgeon makes its appearance. This providential sturgeon has seen the hand drop into the river; it swallows it with well-known voracity, but in the anticipation of re-storing it, seven years later, uninjured to the true owner, and thus to prove her superhuman virtue. And this really happened seven years after the oc-currence in Rome, in the presence of the Pope and his assembled Cardinals.

At first sight it does not appear quite clear, how the sturgeon could have passed from the waters of the Rhine into those of the Tiber, but in this kind of stories there is no use in trying to comprehend everything.

The noble lady and the sturgeon have furnished the theme for the famous novel, " La Manekine," and later, in the Middle Ages, for a great dramatic mystery on the French stage.

Before concluding this chapter, I may be allowed to say a word about the *World of the Dead*, which sends in certain consecrated nights its representatives to some of the churches, or to silent dinners, and about the *World of Ghosts*, the annals of which have been collected, and the laws of which have been explained by Jung Stilling and Kerner.

These ghosts can imitate all the motions of men, walk, run, and even jump, but they have no power

over material objects; they cannot move a table, a chair, or even a straw. All their united efforts would not succeed in causing the light of a candle

to flicker. We can therefore feel perfectly easy
with regard to these ghosts ; they cannot injure
our furniture, nor draw the knot of our cravat in-
conveniently tight, if they should take a fancy to
make an end of us.

Nor can I keep altogether silence as to the
World of Shadows, still dimmer and less percepti-
ble than the World of Ghosts. I shall therefore
content myself with a single instance, which we
owe to a Dutch legend. The master bell-ringer of
the city of Haarlem, caught at a tavern by his wife
escaped with such extraordinary rapidity that his
shadow was unable to follow him, and remained
hanging on the wall — a fact duly certified by the
signature and seal of the reigning burgomaster, the
aldermen, and other notables of said town.

In spite of such overwhelming evidence one
might be disposed to doubt the authenticity of this
remarkable occurrence, which Hoffmann, I believe,
has used in one of his Tales ; but had not long before Hoffmann, and long before the master bell-
ringer of Haarlem even, the god Fô left his shadow
in some town of Hindustan, instead of his card ?
We try in vain to find anything new under the
sun ; all our most famous myths and all our most
amusing anecdotes have travelled all over India before they reached us.

I might also tell you . . . . but he who tells

everything, says too much. Let us here pause once more, and for the last time. Farewell, reader, and may Heaven keep you sound in body and soul.